Spirits

by

ED STAUFFER

ISBN 978-1-956001-55-6 (paperback)
ISBN 978-1-956001-56-3 (eBook)

Printed in the United States of America

Chapter 1

It was dark. No. Murky, difficult to see through. Was it fog? A mist? Smoke from the fire? No. It was thicker than a mist or a fog or smoke and there was no smell. He could move it aside with his hand, like a curtain. It was cold, he was cold. Why was it so dark yet he could see where he was going? Toward the glow, the fire. The first time she came to him he saw the glow was from a fire which he never saw again. Would it be warm? He thought it was and if a fire, he could get warm. But he never saw a fire after the first time, only the glow of one. He didn't know but he believed her to be there, knew that was where he would find her and she needed him, needed his help. His help to do what? How could he help her? He tried to run but his legs wouldn't move. Were they stuck in something? What? He was in a panic. He had to move before It caught up with him. He didn't know what It was, but knew It was after him. Would try to stop him. Then he was able to move but something appeared, in his way. He believed it was a tree. And there it was, the symbol, an upside down cross inside a circle carved into a rock. The vertical shaft extended beyond the circle. It had two horizontals. One that intersected the vertical inside the circle. The second horizontal intersected the vertical outside the circle. Was the symbol Asian, have a special meaning? What? Why wasn't it carved on a tree? It had always been on a tree. No, the symbol was carved into a rock. He knew he was going in the correct direction, but It was close behind him. Then more rocks, and they blocked his path and his view. He struggled to get around them. It was behind him; would It stop him? Then the glow was gone.

He moved around the rocks and the glow was there. In the distance a faint glimmer of light but the glow was above him. Was the glow in the sky? He had to get to the glow, the fire, to her. She didn't cry out, but he knew, she needed him, needed him to save her. He became aware that he was needed to help her from It, help her get away from It. He had to reach her before It did or she would be lost, lost to him, lost forever. No matter how hard he tried to run he couldn't get closer. Would It reach her before he did? What was It? An unseen evil, he didn't know but he knew he had to get to her before He did, It did. Why did he believe It was a He? He never saw It but he suddenly knew. Knew It was a He and not an It. The glow was failing, fading, suddenly further away. She was further away. Then the glow disappeared. He had come to a huge rock, blocking his progress, but the symbol was there, carved into this big rock. He looked up and saw the faint glow. The glow was back and beckoned to him. Was the glow in the sky? No. The light was on top or on the other side of this rock, not in the sky. Desperate to reach her, he tried to scale the rock. But what blocked his way was more than a rock. He had come to a rock face, the side of a cliff, a mountain. He began to climb. There was ice in the crevices, and it was cold. He was cold. His fingers searched the rock face for hand holds. His hands were cold and bleeding, but he didn't feel pain. He was able to scale the cliff and was going to climb to the top. He focused on reaching the top, reaching her. He was exhausted but he struggled onward and upward. He sweated. The sweat mixed with the blood on his hands and added to the difficulty to scale the rock monolith. His hands would slip but he struggled on. Close to the top, he saw the glimmer of light, it was brighter. He was getting closer to her. He was going to reach the glow, the fire, get to her. He was unable to find further hand holds. His hands ran over the rock as he searched for a crevice his fingers could grab hold of. He couldn't find one. He couldn't go on. He began to cry at the thought of losing her. As he searched for a handhold, he felt he was being pulled down and he slipped, let go of his handhold. He began to slide down the rock. Then he was off the rock, falling freely to the ground. Could he somehow be able to break his fall? In a panic he reached out for the rock, but it wasn't there.

Peter bolted upright in bed before he hit the ground. He was shaking. It had been a dream but seemed so real. He could feel the tears on his cheek. He was sweating but felt cold. Was it because he slept in the nude with the fan directly above his bed and it was on? The weather forecast for Denver last night had been forty-five, the warm spell Denver was experiencing in late October would continue for several more days. If it was so warm, why was he so cold? He tried to shake himself awake and dabbed at his eyes with the sheet as he shivered. He tried to calm down. He continued to remind himself that it was only a dream, but the thought of him falling terrified him. Peter looked at the clock radio on his nightstand, four-forty-five. Could he, should he try to go back to sleep? No. Maybe he would dream again. Better to stay awake. Peter decided that he would get ready for work.

He stumbled to the bathroom, grabbed a large bath towel and draped it around his shoulders. Tried to get warm. It was good that he used an electric razor to shave because he was still shaking. He realized his shaking was not from the cold. It was the dream, and the dreams were happening more often and his sense of urgency and desperation were becoming more intense. Worse, they seemed to be becoming more and more real, putting him in danger. They were affecting his waking life. What would Ms. Schwarz say to this? Why couldn't she help him interpret the dreams? Explain their meaning? Why was he having them? What in his life was causing them? He felt that once he knew, he could face it and the dreams. Was she worth the money he had been paying her twice a week? Maybe she could recommend someone to help him understand their meaning so that he could learn to deal with them. Maybe a sleep specialist, a dream specialist, if there was such a person.

He finished shaving and continued to shake. Was it the cold? He hoped a hot shower would help. He stood under the hot water for almost ten minutes before he could feel the coldness leave and the shaking stopped. He dressed in his bedroom and turned on his bedside radio. The first thing he heard was the morning DJ talk about driving conditions, areas to avoid and then the weather for the day. It was going to be another warm one. The high had stalled out over Denver. Its citizens could expect an unusual, possibly a record breaking high in the high sixties to low seventies today, after last night's mid-forties, but it wasn't going to last. There were reports of snow in the mountains and to stay tuned for early ski conditions at ten. While he dressed, he couldn't get past the heaviness the dream had on him, the panic he experienced when falling off the rock. He made a cup of coffee, skipped breakfast, just sat, and thought about the dream for a while. Last night's dream had a cliff blocking his progress, in previous dreams it had always been trees. Could there be some importance in the change of the newest obstacle? Why couldn't he see what, who his antagonist was, tried to get to her before Peter did? Was his nemesis a He? He had always thought of it as It. Now he believed it to be a Him. Why? Peter liked to think of his opponent as It, not a man he was competing against. Was it a man? He was not sure.

At about eight thirty he willed himself out of his kitchen chair, went out his back door and would go into the garage side door to his car. The sun was shining, and it had gotten light enough to see, and Peter saw his neighbor Jannette, cutting some of the dead flowers around her house and throwing them into a basket. She lived two houses down the street from him on the corner and their back yards touched. She was pretty, no, quite good looking, beautiful. She had long light brown hair, or was it blonde? Where was the distinction? He didn't know and didn't study her hair long enough to decide. Only one way to find out for sure, he would have to ask her he thought and chuckled to himself. He thought of her as a blonde with long well-tanned legs, a fabulous body, a blemish free face and pale blue eyes. More than once he imagined what she would look like undressed. She may be or may not be married. He heard from Jeffery Hancock, everyone called him only by his last name, Hancock, another neighbor, she was getting a divorce. Hancock told him he heard her husband spent too many nights and the weekends with Mary Jane.

Jannette was no longer Mrs. Dillon but Miss., Miss. who? Peter didn't know what her un-married name was and didn't ask Hancock. He would continue to call her Jan, Jannette or Mrs. Dillon until she corrected him. It was possible that she would keep her married name, not go through the hassle of changing it back. Had her divorce become legal? Was she single? He never did see a man at her place, her husband, but he wasn't home during the day. Peter never saw a man on the weekends when Peter was home. Someone was keeping her grass cut. The flower garden and leafy plants, which he believed were weeds, now mostly everything was dead because of the early frosts, had almost surrounded the house and from what he could tell was well maintained. The blue and red berries must have been good for the birds because they all disappeared in one day. Maybe it was she who did all the work in her yard, picked the berries and not the birds. He had seen her cut the grass once and early mornings before he would leave for work more than once he saw her tend to the flowers and plants around the house. When he did, Peter did not pay attention to her plants, but her. She did not have large breasts, but Peter thought about them, would like to see them, feel them. He could see over her bikini top but not far enough to see her breasts. Would she fall out of her bikini top when she bent over, would it slip? He hoped so but it never happened. Why was he so fixated on her breasts? They wouldn't be much different from those of the other women he had known. No. But that couldn't stop him from thinking about them.

This morning she wore a low-cut blouse. Did she go braless? He could not tell and quickly decided not to spend time talking to her and trying to find out. His quick glance in her direction was enough this morning,

This unusually warm morning he could clearly see her and as usual he could see that she looked extra sexy in her cut-off jeans. As usual he thought about what she would look like undressed as she bent over and cut off dead flowers and other plants level with the ground. He was sure that there were men in his immediate neighborhood who believed the same thing. Married or not, they would stray from their marriage bed to spend a night with her. But he was the only unmarried man he knew of locally. Would she have sex with him? Probably not. He was not the best-looking guy in the world, but it didn't stop him from thinking of sex with her the first time he met her. Like most of the women he met, he always thought about sex with them, but he never followed through with any. The idea of having an affair with a, was she a married woman or not, an entanglement, and what it could lead to prevented him from doing so. The thought of her, he believed, would take his mind off the dream. In the past the idea of him and her together would begin to arouse him. Not so this morning. Even if she would, he couldn't. She would be divorced, he believed available. Would he pursue her? Try to get her in bed? No. This morning he just waved to her and smiled. He believed that she flirted with him, could be his imagination. Last week she suggested that they should have coffee some morning since they were both early risers. Where? His place? Her place? A local coffee shop? Did he want to believe that she flirted with him? Could the suggestion lead to something sexual? Or was the invitation just casual neighbor to neighbor talk? Maybe he would meet her husband or her ex-husband to be. Did she flirt with other men in his neighborhood? He didn't know and didn't want to find out. For a moment as he thought about her, he saw her with black hair. He panicked and froze. When he recovered, returned to reality, he did nothing more to acknowledge her call, "Good morning neighbor." He only waved to her. He was afraid of her. He had heard from Hancock that her husband had been running around as well as becoming a pot head. What was there about her that her husband had to look elsewhere? He didn't want to find out. Didn't want to meet her husband or ex-husband to be.

When his neighbor and her husband first moved in next door, almost a half year ago, she was friendly. He saw her occasionally when he was in his back yard or out walking. He always knew she was around because of the perfume she wore. Was it lilac? Lily? One of his assistants, Justine, always brought a bouquet of lilacs in, placed them in a vase on her desk and explained that they told her that winter was over, spring had arrived, and summer was just ahead since they were the first flower to bloom in the spring. But they quickly wilted. When he was young his mother had in her flower garden lilies of the valley and stargazers and he could smell both a block away when they were was in bloom and there was a slight breeze. Her scent wasn't overpowering, like the lilies, just enough to notice and sometimes he wasn't sure that it was present or his imagination. This morning he got a whiff of it. Was it from a lily? Something else he would have to ask her.

She never talked about her husband and again when he thought about it, he remembered he never saw a husband, ex-husband, or any man. She always wore a gold necklace with a cross affixed to it. Peter believed her to be religious and most likely faithful to her husband. Besides, when he first met her, he had Clare in his life and his bed. He knew he would be faithful. He would not let his mind drift and fantasize of sex with this woman regardless of how tantalizing she was. But it had been months now, and today there was no Clare and possibly no husband. No. Forget about her, he thought. There was a more pressing event in his life than having sex with his neighbor, an event that was consuming him, his dreams. Where they dreams? No, nightmares. He was not sure what a nightmare consisted of but was beginning to think of his dreams as nightmares. They frightened him. Upset him and effected his daily life.

After the dreams began he did a lot of research concerning dreams and sleeping. He read what different experts said about either their beliefs or theories. Nothing he read helped, and he could not come to any conclusion about his dreams or his sleeping habits. Peter had been seeing an analyst to help him deal with his breakup with his current girlfriend, but it quickly switched to his dreaming. Could his analyst help him with his dreams, why was he having them, could she help him get past them, find a reason why he was having them?

After his wave of acknowledgement to his neighbor, he hurried to his car and began to drive to his workplace.

Peter believed himself as well-fit, he used to work out twice a week at a local gym but since the dreams began he did it less regularly. He was average looking, thought he ate well, had a beer occasionally, owned his own home at the advice of his tax consultant, and had a good job as a business and cost analyst, two positions combined into one. He was well paid and could come and go almost as he pleased. It was because of him that he directed the medical computer software developing company he worked for into expanding and a successful money-making direction. He convinced his boss and the board of directors, it may be a private company but still had a board to help guide it, to cut out the manufacturing company by buying them out. That done, the next step in the company's expansion was to buy out the distribution company. Both moves meant hiring additional employees, technicians, salespeople, and when a union talked to his company's employees, he suggested a profit-sharing plan to keep the union out. It worked. Since the company was privately owned, there were no stockholders who needed to be convinced, to be pleased, only his boss, the owner of the company. And when his boss heard that Peter was being courted by another company, he gave Peter a very big raise, a profit share equivalent to five percent of the company, a new car every year and wanted to promote Peter to be an assistant vice president in order to keep him. Peter stayed with the company but insisted he stay in his present position with his two assistants.

When he reached his company, he parked his Lexus in his designated parking space and realized that the dream's impact on him had mostly worn off but had worn him out. He was physically drained and tired when he entered the building, said hello to the security guard, Al, inside the door and then to the company's receptionist, Virginia, who liked to be called Ginny. She was attractive and like the other women in his life he fantasized about having sex with her, but neither he nor she ever gave any indication that it would ever happen. She smiled and made sure as usual that he saw the large diamond engagement ring on her finger, letting him know, as well as everyone else, she was off limits. She was only the receptionist but had a degree in business and accounting. She made no apologies to anyone and made it quite clear that she was only temporary and would leave as soon as her husband-to-be landed a good job in computer technology. That was over a year ago. No one wished to hire her as an accountant if she intended to work only for a short period of time, but as his company's receptionist all she had to do was answer the telephone, transfer a call, smile when she welcomed people or direct them to see someone. She was naturally friendly, outgoing with good people skills. He hoped that she would stay. Peter had no firsthand knowledge but had heard that she flirted with several men in the company, but no one could verify that she went out with any of them. He never had a conversation with her other than good morning and had heard from one of his assistants that she was pregnant. Today when she stood, he noticed that she began to show. He grunted, "Good morning Ginny," as he passed her.

When Peter reached his office, he saw his two personal assistants and was greeted by both. He often referred to them as secretaries because his mentor at the business where he interned had a woman working for him who he always referred to as his secretary. His two assistants were parked in front of his office door their desks faced each other with a passageway between them to his office. Their area could be construed as a reception area because on either side of the space there were four chairs and a small table. Justine Walker had been hired first and when he began to take on more and more responsibility in the company, he asked his boss for additional help and Mary Ellen Baker had been added. The two women had been with him for the past several years. Were excellent researchers, worked well together and did most of the research he needed, kept him up to date on what needed to be done, arranged his weekly schedule and arranged for Peter people to meet, or people coming to see him, and took care of any travel and lodging that Peter needed done. They wrote up suggestions and were quite good at critiquing what he wanted said so that the paperwork that he generated was persuasive and on point when he presented it. He saw to it that they were well paid, and they were loyal to him. Justine said, "You don't look too good this morning. Another bad dream?"

All that Peter could do was shake his head yes. He left his door open and called out, "If one of you is not too busy, I could sure use a cup of coffee, black, and then both of you come in here."

In a moment Justine showed up with a cup of coffee from the company's canteen, what everyone in the company called their cafeteria, stopped at her desk and picked up a pad of paper and a pencil and she and Mary Ellen entered Peter's office. When he called them into his office it usually meant they were going to be given a task and should take notes. They saw him in his office chair, eyes closed and in the short time since he arrived, seemed to be asleep. Spread out in front of him on his desk was a stack of papers and a bound pamphlet that explained who and what the company did. Both women had seen the company reports many times before. Justine extended her hand with the cup of coffee and quietly said, "Excuse me sir, here is your coffee."

Peter stirred and took a minute to realize where he was and what he needed to assign his two assistants. He thanked Justine for the coffee and told both to sit. When they were seated and ready to write down what he was about to say, he took a sip of coffee and began. "I've looked over where the company is, what it does and how it can be improved. I want this to be quiet, no one should know. Both of you, begin researching a startup division that will research, create, and manufacture medical equipment. A detailed cost analysis for every item for such a project and a timeline. Who we would have to hire, from the head down to the custodians, equipment that would be needed, are suppliers available and can the division somehow be attached to our current building or is a building nearby that we could purchase? If so where, what would either cost. How large a building? Offices and workspaces for its current personnel as well as for expansion. Whatever we manufacture, how difficult will it be to get government approval and who and how we would go about selling it, directly to doctors, clinics or hospitals and don't overlook selling it abroad. Don't overlook a medical procedure and if it can be tied to our current software development division, that would be an added benefit. Don't overlook a medical manufacturing company that we might be able to buy out. Who would we need to oversee it? Will we need to hire engineers, doctors, researchers etcetera. I know you may have questions that must be addressed or answered. Your work and research will have to ask them or answer them. Any questions?" His two assistants were quiet. Before he dismissed them, he said, "One other thing. I believe it is time you both had an office of your own. You two work well together and I want to keep it that way. Either do it yourself or hire someone to plan where and how this area can accommodate two offices, yours, and mine. Keep it close to mine and your arrangement as it is, that it will or will not include the current reception area. Anyone here to see me would have to pass through your office to get to mine. Maybe you two will need a receptionist. If need be, my office could be made smaller or maybe moved. I hope not." This brought big smiles to both the women's faces. Whether the company would expand in the direction he outlined, it didn't matter, and if their ideas were good, the company could possibly double in size. The task he gave the two would keep them from bothering him for a while, especially Justine. She acted like his mother and he didn't want or need her to mother him. When he first hired her, on more than one occasion she called him son. He had to point this out and told her it was unacceptable. At all times he wanted their relationship and appearance to be and look professional.

Chapter 2

For the remainder of the morning Peter didn't get much done. He had trouble concentrating. The dream continued to come back and distract him. He decided on an early lunch, but not at the canteen. He went outside and got in his car and drove several miles and parked in a small restaurant's lot, not far from his analyst, Ms. Schwarz's office. Since he frequented the restaurant, the manager permitted him to park in the lot for long periods of time. The time when he was at his analyst's. His waitress, Maxie, recognized him and how generous he was and was glad to serve him. He thought that she had a nice behind but was too thin, skinny for his taste. He had a quick lunch and then he slowly worked on a cup of coffee that Maxie was only too glad to keep refilled, and he waited. Waited for his appointment time with Ms. Schwarz. He thought about their last meeting and the hypnotist that she had used. He remembered that they searched his past for the women he dated, a woman with black hair and green eyes. One who needed his help because his analyst believed that Peter's dreams had something to do with a woman in his past. The hypnotist took him back to when Peter began working, back through college, back to when he was in high school, when he first began to take an interest in the opposite sex. Told to remember all that they talked about when he woke up, he now wondered if he overlooked someone, someone who needed his help and he ignored. Someone deep in his subconscious that he couldn't remember even when under hypnosis. Maybe someone before high school. The more he thought about his past, the more he believed that he told both that he didn't know this woman or girl, know a woman who needed his help.

Peter remembered Francine Patroski. Told them about her. He said, "She was my first romance. Was it a romance? I'm not sure. She introduced me to the world of sex. I met her at a party. She was eighteen, a year older than me. I had been asked by Kelly to take her to a birthday party that weekend. It was being thrown by her friend Jodi whose parents were out of town. Kelly's parents knew and liked me and had no problem that I was taking her to a birthday party and was sure I would have her home by her 11:30 o'clock curfew."

He told about the first time and Francine.

Once they arrived at Jodi's, she abandoned Peter and went off with her twenty-year-old boyfriend, Gary. Kelly's parents didn't care for Gary and would not have allowed their daughter to go to a party with him or where she could meet up with him. Most of the party attendees paired up and were off in another part of the house and he believed making out, in the basement dancing or outside smoking. He was alone on the sofa in the living room, drinking a Coke and would wait two hours for the time to leave and take Kelly home.

He set his drink on the side table, leaned back, and believed he would sleep for a while. The party music was coming from the basement and wasn't too loud. He knew that there were several couples in the basement dancing to the music. Eyes closed; he began to drift off. Then he was sure the lights in the room went off. He opened them to check and from the light coming into the room from the kitchen, he saw someone standing in front of him. A girl and he recognized her, Francine. She was a year ahead of him in school, but he knew who she was. She was pretty with short dark black hair, cut short or shaved on one side so that her hair was combed to one side and her head appeared to seem unbalanced. Always had dark liner around her dark brown eyes and a black line outlined her dark maroon lipstick. She often wore a ring through her nose. He saw a tattoo around her neck, barbed wire. He had heard that she was weird, the hair, dark make-up, ring in her nose and tattoo on her neck said it was so. She was a little strange, he didn't know her, but she had a nice figure. Peter had heard his fellow ball players talk about her occasionally; she was a vegan. Was it a slang word for a virgin or some sort of cult? He didn't know and he didn't care, wouldn't ask one of his fellow ball players, because if it was slang for virgin, then he was one also. He never asked any of his friends what the word meant. To most of the seniors on the team he heard them say they would do her if they got the chance, vegan or not. One of the seniors wondered if her hair was really that black. Another responded, "Only one way to find out," which was followed with a "How?" and was quickly answered with "Have to ask her," which brought a round of laughs. Peter laughed also but didn't know why. It wasn't for several years that he understood what his fellow ball player had been saying and why it the response generated a laugh.

He didn't know her and had never talked to her. She was just someone he knew in passing, never believed he would ever have any sort of a relationship with her except a "hi" in passing. In the semi-darkness he smiled at her and told her he was trying to sleep for a while. She didn't say anything but hiked up her skirt and straddled him. Before he could do or say anything, she kissed him, lifted herself higher so that her breasts were in his face. Then she did speak and told him they would feel better without a blouse and bra. He didn't know what to do but he did it, unbuttoned her blouse. He didn't know how she did it, but he thought that he heard a plop, plop as her beasts came out of the bra cups. Peter didn't need any prompting, he touched a breast, kissed it, and took the breast nipple in his mouth and massaged the other, went back and forth between them. He was soon hard. He heard her ask if he had any protection. In his wildest imagination he never could have imagined that something like this would happen, could happen. So no, he wasn't prepared, so he didn't have a condom. Until that moment never thought about a condom or needed one. He was a vegan, a virgin. She moved down his legs, reached between his legs and began fumbling with his fly. In a moment she had him out and he heard her tell him this would never happen again without a rubber. Did she mean that they would do it again? He hoped so as he entered her. He didn't think of it at the time but later wondered where her panties were. After several minutes she got off him and put everything back in place. He saw her take a wad of tissue from her purse, wipe herself off and then took her panties from her purse and put them on. Going to the kitchen she told him she hoped he wouldn't tell anyone about what they had done and that he better wipe off his jeans.

The following Monday he saw Francine in school and as they passed, neither gave any recognition of the other. He spent time on his computer and looked up vegan. He found that she was a vegetarian, had nothing to do with her being a virgin. He could accept that. He never told any of his fellow ball players about his encounter with Francine, they most likely wouldn't believe him anyway, although his friends often bragged about a girl in school they had sex with or almost had. At his high school baseball game on Tuesday, which his school won, he was walking out of the ballpark as it was becoming dark. He would wear his uniform home and have his mother wash it. He heard someone say that she liked a guy in a uniform and asked if he wanted a ride home. It was Francine. He accepted. He had a condom in his wallet and needed it before they even left the parking lot.

Peter found several things about her. She was paranoid about getting pregnant. She was on the pill but still insisted Peter use a condom. She had to look after her four younger siblings, two brothers and two sisters, and more than once said she didn't like kids and would never have any of her own. It was okay with him. Her idea of a vegan was she wouldn't put anything in her mouth that came from something that had eyes. That meant meat and fish were out of the question. Some forms of seafood would be okay, but in southern Colorado it would be limited. Like in the song they had sex almost everywhere, once, and sometimes several times a week. She liked to take him out and then sit on his lap so that he would enter her from behind. But mostly it was in the rear seat of the eight-year-old Camaro that she drove. It was given to her by her older brother Jeff, someone Peter never met. When Jeff was arrested for petty theft he was told by the judge either he could go to jail or join the army. He chose to join the marines.

They didn't try to hide that they were an item and did not go out of their way to hide their relationship. He enjoyed sex with her but believed he didn't love her. If he did love her, he wouldn't have said or done the things he did, would have taken her feelings into account. Did he subconsciously try to get her to leave him? Peter wasn't sure as he remembered his brief courtship. He often took her to a hamburger joint and would order a double burger or a pizza joint where he would order a pizza loaded with meat. She would work on a small salad. After one of their visits to the burger restaurant, Peter asked her as she ate French fries, how could she put the fries into her mouth when she knew potatoes had eyes? She didn't respond to the question. One of her primary foods was cheese. So, he asked her how she could eat big eyed Swiss cheese. Again, no response.

They experimented a lot when it came to sex. He learned what and how to do it, to please her. He didn't remember when or how but they got into oral sex. Peter didn't know exactly what she was asking when she asked him if he would like to kiss it. She explained what she wanted him to do. She especially enjoyed performing oral sex on Peter. She often referred to his penis as his bald-headed friend.

They made no plans for the future and had no idea what they would do in the future. Peter had always planned on going to college but not so Francine. A week before the end of the school year she asked Peter to go to her senior prom. They would be seen together, boyfriend and girlfriend. It was not going to happen. After a night of love making, he casually said that his penis was often referred to as a one-eyed snake. The next day she called him and told him she would not be going to the prom with him. She gave no explanation and hung up. Peter believed that he had made a foolish mistake but believed that they would make up now that school was out for the summer and he returned from a two-week baseball camp. He called her when he returned and was told by her mother, Mrs. Patroski, that Francine had moved to California. He asked for her phone number, but her mother would not give it to him, said she didn't have it. Didn't know where in California Francine was living. How would she call her daughter? She wouldn't and told him Francine called her. He was able to convince her that she should tell her daughter the next time they talked that Peter wanted to talk to her. She never did call. He thought about her but the memory of her faded over the course of the summer. He missed the sex but not so much her. Not only did he not go to her senior prom but in addition he did not go to his prom. Instead, he went to a drive in with two of his fellow hall players.

During his senior high school year and for the first two years at CU he did not date anyone. It was six years later that he was talking to Georgina, a school mate and friend of Francine. He asked about her and was told that she married a cattle rancher in central California, had two kids, a boy, and a girl, and operated a day care center out of her home. He really didn't know her. At the time she may have needed him, but not now. "I never have given any thought to what our future would have been like if we had stayed together nor have I felt sorry that I let her go."

He got up, left a generous tip and walked the block and a half to his analyst's building, entered and took the elevator up to the fifth floor and exited the elevator to his right. Her office was in an upscale modern building, but her office did not reflect the architecture of the building. The office had a warm and homey feel, pictures on the wall of smiling people usually with children, overstuffed furniture, and warm incandescent lighting. He believed it was to put her patients at ease and feel safe. The door to her office only had a number on it and her professional name, Dr. Jane Schwarz. Others on the fifth floor had doctor's names and specialties. There was no indication as to what she did. To his left at the far end of the floor was a medical clinic, all the doctor's names and titles were on a board outside. There was even a lawyer and a dentist on this floor. He found all of this out on his first visit when he wandered up and down the hallway, hesitant over entering Ms.

Schwarz's office. As he walked toward her office he again thought about the hypnotist's recommendation during his last visit. He was unable to reveal anyone from his past that would help explain his dreams.

He gave one rap on the door and then opened it and entered an anti-room and sat on the sofa. In a moment Ms. Schwarz came through a door from her office interview room and invited him to follow her. Peter didn't know and never asked why she didn't have a receptionist. He sat in a chair opposite her. She was an attractive forty something with no outstanding features. She was always pleasant and easy to talk to. He never thought about sex with her. He found her name in the yellow pages and called her, made an appointment and had been seeing her now for almost four months. She had been unable to help him with his dreams. She did not wish to refer to them as nightmares.

He sat and remembered Ms. Schwarz when she asked, "Is it possible that she needed you, needed you to help her become a normal responsible woman, give up on what you considered weird?"

He thought about what his analyst had asked him and replied. "Maybe, but from what I heard from her friend; Francine found somebody to do just that."

Today she asked, "Any closer to the identity of who or what you are competing against?"

Peter just shook his head no, but it was becoming clearer that something was not after his dream woman. His pursuer was only trying to stop him.

"Can you defeat It, get to your dream woman before It does?"

"I don't know. Never felt that I had to defeat It. More like It won't let me get to her," he explained. He never saw the woman, only felt her presence. After a moment he said, "It is not an It. Last night I thought of It as He."

"But you've never seen It, Him?" She was silent for a moment as Peter shook his head no. She then suggested they examine this new turn of events, "Could he be someone you competed with in your past?"

Peter didn't have to give it much thought before he answered, "No."

"Are you sure? Say or do anything that made you remember? Did he remind you of someone, visually or physically?"

"No. Like her, I felt Him. Didn't have to see Him," he replied.

"Let's take a different approach, could your dreams concern a man, not a woman. You said you've never seen her?"

Could he have been mistaken, it wasn't a woman but a man? Why couldn't it be a man? He remembered that he never knew anyone with green eyes. Nor could he remember anyone in his past that desperately needed his help, whom would be lost to him forever without his help. Could it have been Francine? No. She was happily married now. He considered Martin, in distribution. Peter didn't really know him. He came into the company with the buyout and was introduced to Peter. Martin was in his mid-twenties, dark hair, brown eyes and with a dark complexion. He was suspected of child pornography. Then he was arrested and convicted of it. Peter never gave him much thought and believed he would get what he deserved. The world would be a better place without him. Martin wanted and needed several people to speak in his favor at his sentencing. Peter was one of the people his lawyer contacted, but Peter wouldn't do it, didn't know him. His analyst thought it prudent that he shouldn't speak in favor for the guy. When he thought about the child pornographer, it all occurred months before the dreams had started. It couldn't be him and Peter never felt any guilt about talking in Martin's favor at his sentencing.

"Were you able to think of any additional women in your life after our last session?" she asked. "Maybe someone you were in competition with? Not a man but a woman?"

It was during his junior year in college when he met his second romance, Carole. He only half-heartedly went out for baseball and didn't make the team even as a walk-on. He focused on his business studies and received good grades. Carole was studying to become a nurse. She had been in one of his psych classes and suggested they study together for the final. He asked her out and they made plans to meet up after the end of the semester. After the first date they got along, she was easy to talk to and was fun to be with. But she was no Francine. In his mind he often would compare the two, but he had never seen Carole with her clothes off, see her body and touch it. He wanted to see her naked. What would she look like, be like? They kissed occasionally and made out, but never had gone all the way, had sex. It was during the fourth week of their dating when they had sex. It was in his room and in the dark, Carole didn't want him to see her naked. She didn't seem to enjoy it. Was it possible that it was her first time? Afterward they didn't discuss it and it was quite a while before they did it again. He liked her and it took quite a bit of persuading from him before she would give in a second time. Couldn't they just be friends. The pressure he used finally got her to admit that she didn't like sex much. She admitted that she did like him, liked him a lot but not the sex they had. Could he spend a lifetime with her when she didn't want to have sex with him? He didn't know but began to have doubts. Had Francine caused him to form an opinion of women, what they wanted of him? What he felt he needed from a woman?

She lived in a sorority and when he called her he would tell who answered the phone he wished to talk to Carole. He would be asked, which one? At the time, four girls in the sorority were named Carol. After the first several times when asked who he wished to talk to he answered, Carole with an 'e' on the end of her name. He soon never was asked which Carol because he would say Carol-E.

During the semester he was invited by her to attend several sorority events. The two of them were considered a couple. They had sex only four times. And now summer was about to begin. Promises of keeping in touch and after a soulful goodbye, they parted, he was going to intern with a business in Denver and she was going home to Tennessee. He e-mailed her. She rarely got back to him. She did tell him her computer was stolen. He began to write to her every week, told her about what he was doing and about the internship. She was always busy, and either would not spend time talking to him on the telephone or would not be there when he called. She wrote him twice and called once. She never called him to talk about the messages he left her. Peter felt sure that they were drifting apart and didn't know how to stop the drift but knew they would get back together when school started.

At the end of summer he called her sorority. No, she hadn't returned yet nor by the end of the first week of classes. He went to her sorority. Susan, a friend of Carole's, talked to him and assured him she had not returned. Was she expected? Susan finally told him no. Carole had hooked up with a high school fling and the two of them moved to Atlanta where she was going to finish her last year of school. Susan had been invited to their gay wedding in June. Carole didn't need his help. Several weeks later he received an e-mail from her thanking him for helping her understand she could never be attracted to men, she was gay. She was sorry if she hurt him and was sure that Peter would understand. He never met her friend and Carole never mentioned her, she very easily could have been Peter's antagonist. If she was, she didn't need to stop Peter, she had won. After Carole he had about half dozen casual relationships with women. None were serious until several years later he met Clare.

Ms. Schwarz waited for him to begin. "I had a bad dream last night. So bad, it caused me to wake up."

"Tell me about it," she said. "Was there anything that you possibly could remember that could have related it to your life? Anything different from the others?"

"No," was his reply. "It was the same old, same old, but more intense. The silent plea for help was there and the glow. But it wasn't trees that blocked me this time. It was rocks, then a big rock, part of a mountain bluff and above the bluff was the glow. On the rock face of the bluff, there it was, the symbol. It was carved into the rock. I began to climb, used the symbol as the first step. I was desperate to reach the light." Peter explained and in as much detail as he could remember what last night's dream entailed, especially how he felt that he was being pulled down. He explained that he believed he was trying to be held back by something, being pulled down by It, Him. He didn't want to go in a new direction with his analyst. "How I felt in the dream, I felt when I awoke. I was sweating and cold even though it was warm in my bedroom. My hands were raw and I shook. I was falling, sliding off the high rock, falling and woke just before I would strike the bottom. I'm afraid to sleep again in the event that I will dream again, start where the last dream ended. Maybe be killed."

"We talked about this before. You know that what happens in a dream cannot happen in life, when you are awake," was her response. "If you are hurt, killed in a dream, it is not real. You will not be hurt and definitely not be killed, never wake up. It has been proven that dreams only happen in your mind. Many times, something in your past triggers them. When you are awake somethings may happen that you believe is a dream, but not the other way around."

His analyst was a bit puzzled by the fact that Peter had reported to her that upon more than one occasion when he dreamed, the dream would be an extension of his previous dream. It would take up where the last one ended. Like a TV episode of a series. This was truly extraordinary. People often could have a recurring dream, but not one that would be a continuation of a previous dream.

The dreams began about four months ago. He wasn't sure, sometime in early or mid-June, shortly after his return from his vacation to Florida and his break-up with Clare. His analyst believed his dreams had something to do with the women in his life, one woman. Did he meet a woman in Florida that he was attracted to? Think about? No. His analyst felt the dreams had to do something with Clare or what she represented, a lost love. But no. The first bad dreams he experienced, he was still with Clare and believed he was in love with her.

At first he never gave the dreams much thought. They occurred about twice a week, sometimes three times. It wasn't long before he realized that they were somehow tied together. They began to have a central theme. An unseen woman needed his help. They weren't intense and many times he would remember them only when some event during the day would trigger them. Was it Clare? Was it another woman in his past? He knew no one in high school, college or work that fit the woman's description. Peter didn't know what she looked like. He had never seen the woman in his dreams, she didn't remind him of anyone he had known. He knew two things about her. She had long black hair and emerald green eyes. He didn't know how he knew; he just did. He and his analyst searched his past for such a woman, or girl. The reason she called in a hypnotist was to find if Peter was hiding some part of his past. He had known several women with dark, maybe black hair, but knew no one with green eyes. They searched for what either could stand for, be a metaphor. What in his life could they be associated with? They could find nothing. They dismissed the dark hair and concentrated on the eyes. Why were they green? Why did he call her eyes emerald green since he had never seen them? Did the emerald have anything to do with his past? How about other gems? Could it be the diamond he had bought for Clare? No. Ms. Schwarz believed that something in his past, something he couldn't remember triggered the dreams. As diligently as they searched his past, they found nothing.

On nights when he didn't dream of trying to reach her, he awoke with a strong feeling that the woman needed his help. He wouldn't dream of her, but he woke with the feeling that she had called to him and the feeling would stay with him for most of the day.

When they had talked about the most recent dream to no avail, Ms. Schwarz changed subjects. "How are you and Donna getting along?" Peter didn't answer her. How could he? Did he want to? Yes. That was the purpose of meeting with his analyst. Donna had dark brown hair, brown eyes and Peter knew no reason that she needed help for anything in her life. "Will she be able to fill the hole in your life when Clare left?" Ms. Schwarz asked.

"No. Donna and I are not together any longer. And Clare didn't leave. I left her and she didn't leave a hole," was his response, "and it has been months since we parted." In the beginning Peter couldn't, wouldn't talk about Clare. Was she the reason he began to see the analyst? Yes. But his dreams began before he left Clare and soon became the focal point of his analysis. Clare soon became a side bar. What did he do wrong with Clare? She reminded him of Francine, and he believed he loved her, wanted to marry her, have a life with her, a family. When they parted, he was surprised at how quickly he was able to get over her, like with Francine. He believed that Ms. Schwarz had helped him, but the dreams began, and his analyst was unable to help him.

He met Clare in a mall almost a year ago. He had been Christmas shopping for his two assistants, was tired and sat on a bench near a fountain. The bench was close to a Victoria's Secret store when this very attractive young lady sat down beside him. Her name tag said Victoria's Secret and her name was Clare. She immediately began to talk about how busy the store was, and she needed a break. She was sorry to unload on him but needed to tell someone or she would explode. After a moment she asked him what he was doing in the mall. After he explained that he was buying two gifts for his two assistants, a necklace for Mary Ellen and a bracelet for Justine, she introduced herself, told him her name was Clare and said it would be nice for him to buy them each an expensive bra and panty set. He was surprised at the suggestion. He knew his assistants well, but not that well and didn't believe that they were on intimate enough terms for such a suggestion. Justine was old enough to be his mother and Mary Ellen was married with three kids, plus, he didn't know their sizes. It was getting late and he told her she only had to hang in there for a short while until the mall closed. She wasn't aggressive but he believed forward when she told him she could do it, hang in there as he said, if she had something to look forward to after work. Peter was about to let it go at that, wish her a good day, or evening, and was ready to leave when she suggested that maybe he could wait around and meet up with her, have a drink. That was how their romance began. They met at a local bar restaurant attached to the mall and they began dating. After their second date, he had her in bed. He was smitten by her, believed he loved her after two short weeks. He often thought of her as Francine. Several months later he was sure he was in love, ready to make a long-term commitment. She knew he had a good job and made a lot of money but had never asked him for anything. But he spent a lot of money on her, bought her things, took her places. They planned on a two-week vacation to Florida during her time off in June. Many times when they ate out, she would insist on paying. She bought him nice things. He thought too nice and expensive on a salesgirl's salary. When he commented on it, she would always say it was nothing. And she would model some of the items her store sold. He liked to see her unclothed and wearing sexy undies. Without trying she was able to turn him on, make him want her. Peter asked her several times to move in with him, but she insisted on staying in her own apartment. She would spend the night with him, sometimes the weekend, but would not let go of her apartment. Was it her touch with her independence as she often said? It was the first week after their return from their vacation in Florida that he had his first dream. He dreamed of a woman pleading for help. Peter didn't see her, but he moved toward the silent voice and put out his hand to help her. But she wasn't there. He grabbed nothing. He thought of it as an unpleasant dream that he soon was able to get over. Later in the week he had a second dream. The same call for help. The woman wasn't there. It unsettled him a little when he awoke but like the first, was easy to forget, shake off.

It was the end of July and Peter had to leave Denver and fly to New York City and meet with a distribution company he and his boss had been talking to, thinking of merging, a buyout by his company. His company made an offer and both company's lawyers were in negotiations. He and his lawyers were to meet with them and their lawyers. The long weekend turned into a one-day meeting, the new company had already made the decision to sell and except all Peter's company's conditions and according to his lawyers it was a good deal and Peter agreed. All that he needed to do was sign off on it. He decided to surprise Clare. In New York he purchased an expensive diamond engagement ring. They had talked about marriage but had not committed themselves to a specific time. He was going to ask her to marry him. She would have to commit herself. He was happy and excited about the prospect. On the evening of the day he left, he returned. He had a key to her apartment, so he was going to surprise her even though they had an understanding that he was to never surprise her, just drop in. But tonight was different, special. He quietly opened the door and entered a dark apartment. Light was coming from her bedroom and he headed for it. He thought he heard her say yes, she most likely was on the telephone. What he saw was like a sledgehammer had hit him in the stomach. His legs gave out from under him and he would have fallen to the floor if he hadn't been leaning against the door frame. On her bed was Clare, naked, eyes closed, being pleasured by, by whom? He didn't know. He had never seen the man before and Clare kept repeating yes, yes, the same way she called out with him. The man turned to him and asked, "Who the hell are you?"

He saw Clare open her eyes and he heard an, "Oh no!" He saw her pull away from the man and said, "Peter, it's not what it looks like."

What could, should it look like? He turned, stumbled toward the door, and left the apartment. Downstairs he threw up. He started to walk to, to where, he didn't know where. Just so that he was walking. Eventually he was stopped by a policeman who believed that he was drunk and taken to the nearest police sub-station. He had trouble focusing but eventually was able to convince the police that he was not drunk or high. He had witnessed his girlfriend with another man. They felt sorry for him and drove him to his car. Clare never called, tried to explain what had happened. He called her and was blamed for not respecting her privacy. She never wanted to see or hear from him again. Peter accepted it as what it was, what he saw. If she had cared for him, could she dismiss him that easily? He had trouble getting her off his mind and out of his heart. And that was when the dreams became more frequent and encompassing. That was when he contacted Ms. Schwarz and began seeing her, but only once a week which soon turned into twice a week. He needed help dealing with his break-up with Clare, not with his dreams. He came to the realization with his analyst's help, that on the nights that she wanted to be alone it was because she was not in love with him but was with another man. Maybe someone she loved. She was not trying to keep her independence; it was because she was seeing someone else. She broke his heart until he realized how gullible he had been. Ms. Schwarz helped him see that it was only infatuation, not true love. That was when Peter brought up the dreams of an unseen woman. Peter didn't know who the woman was that needed his help and he was stressed by, by what? He didn't know, but he was stopped from reaching the woman. His first thought was that it could be Clare, had to be her. If it were her, why couldn't he see her. Was it her true love who was trying to stop him from getting to her?

In a weak moment he called Clare again. This time as soon as she knew it was him, Clare hung up. She wouldn't talk to him, made it quite clear that she didn't want to hear from him again. Everything he thought was between them, it was only him, his belief. It was never Clare. She didn't want or need him. He believed he had been a means to an end. And that end was to have a good time and enjoy sex with a man, any man. Ms. Schwarz got him to remember that he did all the talking about love, marriage, and a family. It wasn't something that they talked about; it was something he talked about. No. He had been the other guy in her life. The guy she cheated with. It didn't take long for him to get past Clare, but not past the dreams. They were becoming more frequent and grew in intensity. They frightened him.

He returned to what the two of them had been discussing, Donna. "I'm not seeing her."

"Did the two of you have a fight so soon?" his analyst asked. "Could it possibly be because she was married once?"

"No, to both," Peter replied.

"She wouldn't sleep with you?" Ms. Schwarz asked.

Peter hesitated before he answered. "Just the opposite."

"Explain," she prompted.

Again, he hesitated before he was able to get out, "She wanted to, but I couldn't."

"Did you feel that you didn't know her well enough or long enough? Out of respect for her?" his analyst asked. When he didn't immediately respond, she followed up with, "It is nothing to be ashamed about, it will eventually happen between the two of you, nothing to cause a rift in your relationship."

He told her everything about his past, what he had done with the other women in his life and with Clare. She never passed judgement on him, so why stop talking to her now. "I believed we would make love. I had her undressed and in the dim light in my bedroom she looked beautiful and I wanted her. But then it happened. I couldn't perform. Couldn't keep an erection. I tried, and so did she, to get me excited, nothing. In my mind I heard the overpowering silent plea for help. I believed I was betraying the woman in my dreams. I heard, no felt, why was I leaving her? I was startled and it took me a second or two, but I answered her. Donna thought I was talking to her when I asked, "Who are you? Where are you?" Then I felt that I was answered. "You know who I am. You know where I am." I was in a panic. I didn't know who she was or where she was. We eventually got dressed without saying a word to each other and on the drive to her place she said she was sorry. Sorry that she wasn't woman enough for me. She believed that we should stop seeing each other. I didn't respond. How could I tell her that the woman in my dreams wanted me, needed my help, was now coming to me in my waking life." He paused before he said, "My dreams are interfering with my everyday life."

"What about your good-looking neighbor. Do you still, as you once said, lust after her?"

"No. For a moment I thought she had black hair this morning. I'm beginning to see things that are not real," he said. "Not even in her low-cut blouse and tight cut-offs could she stir me, cause me to have lewd thoughts."

"You said you believed she was getting a divorce. Will you pursue her?"

Peter was sure that he wouldn't. He didn't answer his analyst but shook his head no.

Ms. Schwarz followed up with, "But for now, your time is almost up, we will continue during your next session. Until then, I want you to think about, do you ever feel alone when you are alone? It's been months now since you broke up with Clare and according to you, you have not been with another woman except for Donna since. Is this correct?"

All that Peter could say was, "Yes."

"Before you leave," Ms. Schwarz continued, "I believe that you should continue to see Donna, work it out with her. Maybe you need a woman in your life. You can't be alone. You told me there were only short stretches of time in your life that you were alone. You were always with women, maybe not sexually, but you were not alone."

Peter thought about what she said and didn't have a response. After a moment of silence Ms. Schwarz said, "I told a college friend who is into foreign customs, beliefs and religions about your dream symbol. I thought it might shed some light on your dreams. It is not an Asian symbol. She told me of a vague reference to something else. A small cult of devil worshipers in Eastern Europe during the fifteenth century used a symbol close to it. Many in this cult were considered witches and were burned at the stake. Fewer and fewer of them believed in devil worship and followed the cult's beliefs. They didn't want to be thought of as witches in consort with the devil. The cult died out and so did their belief."

"Why are you telling me about this?" he asked.

Ms. Schwarz hesitated before she answered. "Do you believe in reincarnation?"

The question by his analyst caught him completely off base. He didn't have to think about it. "No" he said emphatically. "When you are dead, you are dead. Why do you ask?"

"There is a growing number of people, some professional, who dabble with the idea. There is absolutely no truth or evidence that anyone has lived a previous life. If you did, were reincarnated from an ancient cult, it would not be out of the question that an ancient lover is calling to you. Someone you don't remember."

Peter thought about it for a moment and answered, "No. I am not reincarnated, a devil worshiper, in consort with the devil."

Later that day he was intrigued by what his analyst had said. Could he have been reincarnated? No, but it did not stop him from pursuing the subject on his computer. What he found surprised him. There was a "life after death" group in Denver. He called and was informed that the group would meet that night. All previous lifers were welcome.

After work he had something to eat at a restaurant and drove to the address. He saw a non-descript house in what he thought was a poor neighborhood. His first impression was that the houses were seedy, in need of repair or paint. Many had various pieces of litter, junk in the yards, over gown grass lay flattened by the recent snowstorm.

Peter was welcomed into the house by a middle age man and when he entered, he saw that the interior did not live up to the exterior. It was dark, lit by candles. A mist from burning incense filled the air and it was chilly. Over a dozen chairs were arranged in a semicircle oriented toward what could best be described as an altar and most were occupied by a person. He was seated and in about ten minutes the meeting started. There was testimony of previous life experiences that lasted for well over forty five minutes. None of what he heard could be proved, and for this group, disapproved. Were they telling of a previous life's experience or what they liked to have happened? Peter listened to what was said but dismissed it as something that could have happened. The time, place, special events that took place and clothing that was described could all have been found on the internet.

The meeting finally ended and people began talking to each other or headed for the door. Peter was met by the older man who greeted him upon his entrance. "I see you are new, want to know more about your past. I'm Jimmy-Jay and I, for the most part, run this club. Members pay twenty dollars a month dues. Are you interested in joining?"

"No, not really. I thought I could learn more about reincarnation but all I heard was people talking about their past life."

Jimmy-Jay hesitated for a moment before he said, "That is what reincarnation is, you having lived before. Do you believe you have lived in the past? Have been reincarnated?"

"No. I want to know if someone from my past is trying to contact me, comes to me in my dreams."

"We are about previous living, not trying to be contacted by someone from a past life. Me for example, I was a slave in ancient Rome."

There was no mention of what had happened to Jimmy-Jay between the time he lived as a Roman slave up until today, so after a moment Peter said, "I don't believe that you can help me. Thank you for letting me attend your meeting," and he turned away and began to head for the door.

"Maybe you do have a previous life experience. Let me give you something that may unlock your past." He held out his hand and gave Peter a small plastic bag of what? Peter didn't know or if he should take it, but he finally did. "Boil this herb and try to inhale the vapors, when it is cool, drink it. It will help unlock your past. I hope to see you next week."

That night Peter did what he had been instructed to do with a small amount of the herb. It smelled awful and tasted worse. He got nothing from it except for a slight buzz and it burned his tongue. There was no bad dream that night. The next day he took the herb to the research facility head in his company, Bruce, and asked for a detailed analysis of the substance. His explanation was that he was to take it to clear his sinus problem. In the afternoon he received a call from Bruce. "From the best that can be determined it is made up almost entirely of tea, Tetley I believe. It has a strong lacing of THC, a small sprinkling of what appears to be nothing more than baby powder and what gives it a bad taste is finely ground salt, tarragon, and a derivative of a hot pepper, Caroline Reaper I believe. It can have no purpose other than to be hot, taste bad and possibly get you high." So much for someone trying to reach him from his past, possibly a witch, and so much for the 'life after death' club. He dismissed the idea of reincarnation that his analyst had planted in his brain.

Chapter 3

That night he dreamed about his unseen woman and she needed his help but only the plea for his help. He didn't awake in a panic. The only good thing about the morning was that when he was leaving, he didn't encounter his neighbor. Arousing or not, he didn't wish to see her and the possibility of seeing her with black hair.

The look on his face told his two assistants that his night did not go well. Both knew about the dreams that he had been having and that he was seeing an analyst. They didn't know just how bad they were becoming and how they would be affecting his work. Both hoped that his analyst would be able to help. Neither said anything but nodded to him when he showed up for work.

Peter thought about the symbol in his dreams as a symbol used by devil worshipers. Witches. In his waking life he had never seen the symbol. His first thought was that it was the symbol for women, but it was not complete. Could it have come from the centuries old symbol for devil worshipers and over time the cross in the center was left off since most witches were thought of as women? Peter could come up with several reasons for the symbol, but they were all guesses, assumptions on his part. He wasn't very religious but for sure he never thought about being in league with the devil. He didn't know if the devil or God even existed. He didn't believe in the super-natural, never would he have thought about someone reading his palm or predict his life's outcome by checking his birthday and his astrological sign. Nothing in his life could he connected to such an incidence.

He forgot about the symbol in his dreams and thought about what Ms. Schwarz said about getting back with Donna. Should he call her? Apologize? Apologize for what? That he was not the man she needed in her life. He couldn't love her. No. They parted so it was best he leaves it at that. They should never have met. It was an accident. Or maybe it wasn't.

It had been late in the afternoon when he got a call from the company's accountant, Janet (JC) Crowne. She was not going to be able to meet with the catering manager to finalize the company's banquet needs, would Peter do it? The banquet wouldn't be that costly and it was a way to benefit, reward the company's employees. When he thought back on it, was it a plan of JC's to have him meet this manager, Donna Feleze. Justine, on more than one occasion, mentioned a single woman in the company who was pretty, single, and not dating anyone. Would Peter think about asking her out? Could his two assistants have conspired with JC to have him meet this woman, Donna Feleze, the company's caterer for the banquet? It didn't matter. If they did, he felt sure that they believed it was for his benefit. But if they had, he wished they hadn't.

At Donna's place, which did large scale catering, especially for large weddings, he was shown to her office. He was introduced to a slender and attractive young woman, dark brown hair, brown eyes, and a nice figure. He wondered what she would look like undressed and in his bed. Would he try to find out? No. JC had called her and explained that she couldn't make their meeting and was sending a company co-worker who would take her place. He would have to sign off on it anyway. The estimated attendees for the banquet were twelve hundred, give or take a few. All three branches of the company had a total of five hundred and eighty-three employees, all could bring a spouse or other, and members of the family. No children under eighteen. Part of the distribution branch located in New York that had only recently been acquired were invited, but it was expected that none from New York would attend. The cost was going to be somewhere just north of fifteen dollars per person, plus there would be several hundred dollars for tipping the servers. It seemed irrelevant to him, but shouldn't that be included in the total cost and not a separate item, the DJ was. She told him the server tips would be bundled into the total cost at his request. He and Donna came to what seemed an agreeable amount total for the food that would be provided, flowers on the tables and tablecloths. JC had made arrangements for a hall, tables and chairs, and an open bar. Each attendee would be provided with two tickets that would allow them to two adult drinks. Soft drinks and water would be free. The bar bill would also be added and bundled into the total cost, but if it exceeded the estimate total, an additional bill would be sent to his company. He was ready to leave when Donna told him to wait a moment and she talked into her phone. After a short time, the door to her office opened and a woman in a chef's uniform entered pushing a covered cart. She uncovered the cart to show an assortment of food. He was to sample it to see if it met his expectations, it did. He signed the contract with Donna and the bill would be sent to JC.

At the banquet, many praises were given to an assortment of people. Near the end Donna showed up, saw Peter at a table and joined him. He was flippant with her when he asked if he could buy her a cup of coffee since servers had put coffee carafes on each of the tables. She said yes and so it began. She had no idea who Peter was or what he did for the company until the very end of the banquet. The company's president said to conclude the night's festivities, there was one last but special person to be recognized and thanked. The company had a very good year and this person, Peter Frost, should stand. "He should be thanked for the banquet and because of his guidance, will be recognized in your next paycheck. Everyone will be receiving an early Christmas present, a bonus, twenty-five percent of your monthly salary." Peter got a standing ovation that lasted for five minutes and afterwards many pats on the back and thank you's. He saw Donna helping the serving staff collect dinner ware, napkins, and glasses, didn't think anything of it and left with others. It was on Monday that Justine told him how wonderful the banquet was and the excellent food. He should give the manager a call and thank her. He did and asked her if he could really buy her a cup of coffee. At first, they were just friends and found out a lot about each other. It was two weeks later when the incident occurred. Not enough time for them to become too involved with each other, especially sexually, and so easy to walk away. She had invited him to have Thanksgiving dinner at her place which was never to happen.

He did not call Donna, as Ms. Schwarz had suggested, and he thought about how he felt being alone. He was alone but he never gave it much thought. He never felt lonely, believed it was a state of mind and didn't seek out others to be with. He believed himself to be happy, satisfied with life until the dreams, the nightmares began.

They occurred weekly. Sometimes more and sometimes less often. They were nestled between the pleas for help. They were not desperate, just pleas that during the day would come back to him and except for bothering him did not cause a panic. They were not dreams but the feeling of pleas from his dream woman. The dreams that caused him to panic were the ones he referred to as dreams that he now referred to as nightmares. This night was several days since the last dream and as usual Peter was afraid to go to sleep that night, but he finally did, and he slept through the night. He assumed that the hypnotist suggestion that he should sleep well at night, not have any dreams that would trigger an anxiety attack had worked and he did not have a feeling of a plea for help. Why hadn't his analyst and he tried this sooner? The same for the next several nights. When he told this to Ms. Schwarz she believed that they were making progress and even though they could find no reason for the dreams, the hypnotherapy was working. He had begun to look at his life and felt it wasn't so bad. It was what the dreams were trying to tell him. He didn't want or need others. Didn't need to help the woman in his dreams. She was not his responsibility. And the being pursuing him? If he were not going to try to help the woman who needed him, well, the being wouldn't exist either. Peter was feeling good about himself.

Sunday night he fell asleep on his sofa while watching a football game. Suddenly something was pulling him to the edge of the cliff and then he was falling, sliding down the rock. It was the same rock he had fallen from before. He feared he would be killed when he hit the bottom. He frantically grabbed out, hoping he could find a hand hold that would slow him down, break his fall. His hand reached out, came in contact with something on the rock face and he grabbed it. The shock of the sudden stop startled him, and he felt as if his arm was about to be torn off. He was afraid, shaking with fear, but he was alive. He was sure he could feel something running down his arm. He looked and saw it was blood. His feet could touch ground at the bottom. He let go of what he had grabbed and saw it was the symbol, higher on the rock face than when he first saw it. It was bloody now. He was alive. He looked at his arm and his hand. The hand was bloody, and he had trouble lifting his arm. He had hurt it in the fall. And then it came to him, the silent plea for help. He believed he heard her tell him that he was so close. He looked up and thought he saw something, large and dark. What was it? He didn't know but It/He was what pulled him down the rock face. He couldn't help her, his arm was hurt and whatever it was, stood in his way. He regretted he wouldn't be able to save her, but he had to leave her, leave her to her fate. He began to wander, back through the rocks and then they turned into trees. He had no idea where he was going, he was just going. He knew his hand was cut and his arm was hurt but he couldn't feel either. He kept wandering through the trees. And then he saw in the distance the warm glow. Not above on the rocky cliff, but ahead beyond the trees. It was her. He was moving toward her. Could he reach her, help her? He knew he would try. Must try. He got closer, the light brightened, it seemed to be shining through a cloud, a cloud close to the ground. The cloud seemed to change shape brightened to the point that he couldn't see. In the light he believed he saw a face, but it wasn't a face. It reminded him of, of what? He didn't know. No one he recognized, but it wasn't a face, it only reminded him of one and as he continued toward it, it seemed that its mouth opened and he would be swallowed. It didn't have any teeth. It was only a hole and the light came from it.

He awoke with a jolt. He had been dreaming. He couldn't shake the idea of the menacing face, he was sweating, and his arm hurt. Had he slept on it wrong? That was his first thought, his arm was asleep. He waited for a moment and then grabbed it with his other hand and moved it. When he did, he cried out, "Oh no!" Not only did it hurt but his hand was bloody. What he had dreamed had happened. There was nothing on or around the sofa that could have caused what he felt and saw. He was in a panic.

Fight the panic he thought, calm down. It couldn't have happened. Somehow before he fell asleep, he had hurt himself. Where? On what? Peter couldn't come up with answer. The more he thought about it the more he shook, shook with fear. Fear of the unknown. This couldn't, shouldn't have happened. If he hurt himself in his dream was it possible that the being, the face in his dream could materialize in his life? What could he do? He dialed Ms. Schwarz's home phone number. It was three o'clock in the morning, he didn't care. When she finally answered the phone, he told her who it was calling her this late at night and he had to see her right away. He had another bad nightmare and had hurt himself. He heard, "If you are seriously hurt, call 911." He said he wasn't. He told her he had hurt his arm in his dream and when he woke it was sore and his hand was bleeding. She was able to calm him down and told him, "I'll meet you in my office at seven o'clock. In the meantime, you should try to stay calm, take some aspirin for the pain and take a hot shower. Try to relax."

Her advice helped. Peter was able to meet her at her office. She patiently listened to him as he talked about last night's dream. His analyst did not have an answer as to why the dreams, especially the fact that this dream started where the last one ended and the blood on his hand and the sore arm, again she was perplexed. And now a new element had been added to his dreams, a face. Peter told her it wasn't a face but reminded him of a face-like shape. Could the face hurt him? No. It was only a dream. But he had hurt himself in his dream which was real when he awoke. Was it possible that he had gotten up in his sleep, hurt himself and returned to the sofa? He didn't think so. He had no remembrance of ever sleep walking and all the people that he had spent time with never said that he did.

He told his analyst all this when they met that morning. Ms. Schwarz made a call and in a short time ushered him down the hall to the clinic at the end of the hallway. The first thing he had to do was give the receptionist his insurance card. After a few moments she introduced him to one of the clinic's doctors. The doctor introduced himself, but Peter didn't hear or care that he didn't catch his name. She related why they were there, and Ms. Schwarz watched as Peter was examined. The doctor said the blood came from under two of his fingernails and was the reason Peter could see no wounds. How could he have cut himself under his fingernails when he was asleep on his sofa? He didn't tell this to the doctor. The doctor felt Peter's arm and Peter told the doctor where and when it hurt as he was touched. An x-ray followed, but the doctor said he could find nothing wrong. The pain most likely came from Peter sleeping on it wrong. There was nothing that could be done for it and Peter was told to use it as little as possible and the doctor wrote out a prescription for pain pills. If it didn't get better the doctor said he could arrange for Peter to see a physical therapist.

Back in her office Ms. Schwarz also wrote out a prescription for Xanax. It hopefully would help control his panic attacks and she recommended an over the counter sleeping pills. Had he ever considered marijuana? She believed that it would relax him and less susceptible to dream panic. Maybe he would also be able to sleep more soundly. He believed he would need something that would calm him down immediately when he would awaken. He had tried smoking marijuana in college and didn't care for it much. Yes, he would try it if the Xanax didn't work but he didn't hold out much hope for it.

Peter had calmed down as he talked to her. Ms. Schwarz suggested that he see a dream specialist, someone who might be able to interpret his dreams and may be able to get to the root of his problem. She knew of such a person, Doctor Wesbaumh, a psychiatrist who worked with and researched sleep and people's dreams at his clinic, but he was in San Antonio, Texas. Would Peter be willing to go see him? "Yes," was his response and he waited while she made the call. He listened as he heard her talk to someone on the phone. He told her no to the appointment when she told him he would have to be on site for several weeks, possibly a month or longer.

At his office, his assistants couldn't help but notice the shape Peter was in. His face was red and seemed puffy. After he sat at his desk both entered and laid out in front of him their initial report on the work that they had been assigned, a detailed outline of what needed to be addressed and in what order. He began to look at it but was unable to focus. What he read, he couldn't remember and had to go back and read it again. After five minutes he had only read the first paragraph of the draft and had no idea what it said. He excused himself and went to the bathroom where he washed his face with cold water. He felt better and returned to the two waiting assistants. He told them he would finish reading it later and get back to them. Anything he read now or said would be meaningless. They were ready to leave when Justine asked if he had had another bad dream, a nightmare. Yes, but his analyst said he was making progress and not to be disturbed by it. "Did what she say to you, did it help?" Justine wanted to know.

"No. Not really," was all that Peter could say.

"I probably shouldn't say anything about this, but have you talked to Mary Ellen about your nightmares? Not your dreaming but what was causing the dreams."

Peter didn't know what Mary Ellen could tell him about why he was dreaming when his analyst couldn't. All that he could say was, "No." Why would he? Why should he? He didn't add anything more to the conversation and Justine left his office as he picked up the work they had done and again he began to read. This time he was able to spend more time on it and could see where his two assistants were coming from, it was a three-page detailed outlined approach to the assignment. What Justine had said about talking to Mary Ellen kept gnawing at him. What could she possibly say or do to help him, he wondered, and he dismissed her from his thoughts.

Later that day he returned to what Justine had said. Maybe he should have a talk with Mary Ellen. The slightest reference to anything that could affect his dreams seemed to arouse his interest. The decision made, he went to her desk and found that she had left for the day. Well then, maybe tomorrow he would talk to her, but for right now it appeared that the panic medication that Ms. Schwarz had recommended was doing its job. He did not feel bad and if the sleeping pills she recommended worked, he would be able to sleep, undisturbed. He felt sure the panic medication was working. He had no apprehension about sleeping.

That night he dreamed but was not in a panic when he awoke. His dream picked up where the last one ended. He was walking toward the bright light but there wasn't an image of a face. The light was the sun shining between the trees. There was no desperate silent plea to save her. Then he heard, no felt, not a plea for help, but you're too late. He felt she was gone. If the Xanax made him lose his woman, then so be it.

When he awoke he wasn't in a panic. He wasn't cold or sweating, maybe a bit groggy. He believed it was over, the dreams. Whatever caused them seemed to have reached a resolve. That morning he looked forward to going to work. He didn't know but it promised to be a good day. He didn't pay any attention to the fact that during the day it had snowed more. Winter had moved in. He forgot about talking to Mary Ellen, no need.

He told this to his analyst. The drug was helping. "I've gone back over our meetings and I recognized a pattern, or at the least maybe a pattern. Your most serious dream panic attacks are almost a month apart and then die down and then your dreams seem to build for a month. I've thought about this coincidence and wonder if there could be a reason for that. Could there be a reason for it? What in your life, in this world, could be tied to a monthly occurrence? The only things that I am aware of that occurs on a monthly basis is the changing of the moon and a woman's menstrual cycle. The tides occur daily and other events that happen monthly are the result of something man has devised and can be changed."

Peter thought about what he had just heard and could see nothing in his life that in any way occurred monthly. He was paid on a monthly basis but that could easily be changed.

After a moment Ms. Schwarz said, "If this is more than a coincidence maybe we need to examine the women in your past that this could be connected to. A possible explanation would be that one of the women in your life was pregnant, by you or someone else, and your dreams focus on that. Could you deny the fact you got a woman pregnant? Refused to help a woman get an abortion or maybe the other way around, you did help this woman, and now are being haunted by it? Feel blamed. Feel guilty?"

Peter was completely shocked by what he heard. He shook his head no and after a moment replied, "If what you suggest is even remotely possible, I have no recollection of it. Either I or the women I've had sex with have been careful. I've never been accused of getting a woman pregnant nor have I ever been asked to help or assist a woman get an abortion, possibly pay for one. This idea has never crossed my mind."

"The idea occurred to me when I examined the times you said your dreams were the worse. Think about it and if there is a possibility let me know and we will examine it as a cause."

Peter did think about it and was able to dismiss it as something that occurred to him in the past. After Francine and Carole how many women were there? To date until he met Clare, he could only remember six others. They had always been short term, one or two nights. None of them tried to get in touch with him or date him again. And the moon, it may change monthly but how was it possible that it could in any way affect him. He soon dismissed what his analyst had suggested.

Chapter 4

For the next several days Peter had dreams about the woman who needed his help, but they were not bad, the pleas for help were not desperate, nor did they panic him. Christmas came and went. He had been invited to several parties. He went to several and found that he shied away from any single women he met at them. It was easy to stay home, light his gas fire in his fireplace and just veg-out. He was called one evening before Christmas by his neighbor Jannette and asked if he would be a reference for her, she was applying for several jobs. He said yes but was not sure what he could say about her, but he never had to because Peter never heard from her again nor any company that wished to hire her. In fact, he hadn't seen her for quite a while. Maybe she did get a job, or maybe after the divorce, she moved. He didn't send Christmas cards, but he did receive several. One was from her. Maybe she hadn't moved. He went outside to check the snow on his drive and sidewalk. The lawn and tree service he had hired on a year-round contract usually did a good job removing it. He hoped that he might see her. Did he miss her? Peter thought about it and was not sure why he missed her. No, she bad just become a part of his mornings. Today no such luck but, she or someone had been shoveling the snow from her walk and driveway.

He felt good enough that he reduced his analyst times to once a week. He no longer needed the panic medication that Ms. Schwarz had prescribed since the intensity of his dreams seemed to have lessened, but he discontinued to use the sleeping pills. He always felt listless and a bit groggy the next day and had trouble concentrating. The sleeping pills did not stop him from having dreams about his unknown woman, his dreams were not bad, bad enough to cause him to be in a panic when he awoke. When he thought about it, Peter did not have trouble sleeping, it was about the nightmares he had when he slept. The bad dreams usually occurred prior to when he woke. No, the dreams caused him to wake. Did he sleep well before the dreams? Yes. Did he try to sleep after the dreams caused him to wake? No. He didn't because he believed the dreams would continue. He had not wished to find out.

It was almost three weeks since his last bad dream about her, his unseen and unknown woman, and he believed the dreams were over. They had been replaced with pleasanter dreams, dreams about fishing, but it was close to a month since the last bad one. He remembered what his analyst said about the dreams being worse on a monthly cycle. Should he be concerned? No. He felt the medication he was taking had helped.

Peter had mentioned fishing in passing several days before Christmas to a fellow worker. He thought about taking up trout fishing again. He had done it when he was younger and had heard of the native brook trout in several mountain streams. They could be very challenging, but he was willing to spend time in the mountains pursuing them at either of his past two favorite fishing streams, Wild Bear Creek or Shay's Run. His two assistants had heard his remark, did some research, and bought him a new bamboo fly fishing rod and a reel to go with it for Christmas. In his mind he began to count down the days until the snow melted and he could go fishing. He had rummaged around in his garage until he was able to find his old pair of fishing waders. They hadn't been used in well over ten years and upon inspection, he saw that they showed several fine crack lines, but he would try them on as soon as water was available and see if they leaked. Every day after Christmas he seemed to be more and more focused on fishing and twice dreamed about fishing in the small, not well fished stream he fished when he was young, Wild Bear Creek. He could clearly remember seeing fish in the clear pools that he fished. It seemed in these dreams, he fished, but never seemed to catch anything.

He was carefully approaching the pool of water formed by a large tree that had fallen across the stream. He didn't want to spook the fish. Too late. One or more fish had caught a glimpse of him, and he could see them scatter in the pool, swimming to the sides or beneath the tree and disappear. He would try anyway. He floated his bait down to the tree and hoped one would be dumb enough to strike at it. No such luck. He began to walk across the stream on the fallen tree. When he was on the tree he looked into the water and he saw fish, frightened by the vibration of his feet, they swam from beneath the tree into the open pool area. May as well try and he dropped his bait into the pool. He didn't feel the line pull, didn't see the fish go after it, but he knew a fish had gone after his bait. When he lifted his rod to catch the fish, that was when he slipped into the pool. The last thing he saw, before he hit the water was the symbol, carved into the tree he had been standing on. What had looked to be only a foot or so deep was over his head. He reached up and grabbed for the tree. It wasn't there and he could not touch the bottom of the stream. He tried to rise in the water and found that his waders were filled with water and held him down. Where did they come from? He hadn't worn them earlier. In desperation he again reached for the tree. In a panic he had let go of his fishing rod and now searched for it. He was unable to find it and he was being pulled down stream. It was no longer the small clear stream that he fished but a muddy raging river. He bounced along, bumping into rocks, and all the while he spit out water. He thought that he could feel the dirt and taste the grime of the river. He struggled to reach and stay on the surface but as soon as he reached the surface he would be pulled down into the water. It seemed that something was pulling him down, not the weight of his waders filled with water. He felt he was about to drown, and then he was above the water and he could breathe. He thrashed in the water until again he was pulled down and water rushed into his mouth. As hard as he tried, he was unable to pull himself free of whatever held him down, reach the surface and air. He was doomed. Then he thought he heard her, her silent plea for help. Why had he abandoned her? Still under the water, he began to cry. He felt her say to him, not in words but feeling, he let her go but she would not let him go. He struggled to get free of the water and he felt that whatever was holding him under the water seemed to let go and in desperation, he reached for the surface. His head broke the surface of the water.

Peter bolted up in bed. He was soaking wet and shaking. The bed was wet, and the woman and panic attacks were back. How was it possible for him to get wet? It was only a dream. Because the dreams were real, he was experiencing them. It was impossible. In some strange way he was entering his dreams, taking part in them. But that was impossible.

He lay in bed and thought about what he had just dreamed, afraid to move. But he was cold. He finally forced himself up and went to the medicine cabinet and he downed two of the Xanax and waited. They soon began to work, he felt better. A hot shower would help.

He was calm but worried. He had to see Ms. Schwarz. She could hear the urgency in his voice. He had to see her today. He was to come in after lunch. He dressed and sat, stared out the window but saw nothing. Everything was white. Had it snowed more last night? He didn't know or care. If it did, his service would shovel his walk and driveway. He did not care to see his neighbor.

He stayed home in the morning. After lunch backed out of his garage and drove to his analyst's building. He told her about his nightmare. "I have no idea how I could have gotten wet."

"Maybe it was sweat?" was her reply.

"I don't think so. It was cool in my bedroom and there was too much. It was water."

Ms. Schwarz didn't know how she could help and suggested he go and see her psychiatrist friend in Texas. Maybe the dreams had nothing to do with his waking life. It could be that there was something that was not right with his brain. Whatever the cause, it was manifesting itself in a dream. Better he dreamed them instead of acting them out in real life. He waited while she made an appointment. She reminded him, "You may be required to be at the dream research clinic for several weeks. Can you get off work?"

"I don't care. I must find the reason for the dreams, what I can do about them. Maybe there is a growth, a cancer, a tumor on my brain. The MRI my regular doctor arranged found no abnormalities that could be the cause of his dreams. I need to find out."

She talked into the telephone and set up an appointment. Peter had given her permission to forward the records of his meetings with Ms. Schwarz. When she was finished, she asked Peter, "Is it possible you got wet before you went to bed and then dreamed about falling in the dream? It would explain the water."

"No," he replied, "I did not get wet," and he paused, "I can't be that forgetful." After a moment he continued, "I'm thinking, not to try to save himself in the dreams when I find himself in danger. Find out if I really would die."

"You most likely wouldn't be able to put into your dream what you thought about in your waking life," was her reply.

"Why not? The dreams are happening to me in my awake life. Why not the opposite? Wouldn't it be possible for me to make my dreams be what I want them to be?" he said to his analyst.

"It doesn't work that way. Dreams are not real," she replied. And as an afterthought she said, "If what you say is true and you die, how will you know?"

He left her office and went to his building. They both agreed that he should stay on the panic medication. He was a little better and thought about what she had said. His brain wouldn't work if he were dead so how would he know? Let some philosopher figure that one out. He quickly switched to his meeting with a specialist in Texas and found himself looking forward to it. Maybe he would be able to help Peter. If he remained positive, maybe the results would also be positive.

Chapter 5

Peter returned to work and called the head of his company and told him of his need to take several weeks medical leave. He was not asked why but was given the go ahead. He would have to clear it with all those working under him or who his absence would affect their work. Justine saw the worried look on his face when he arrived at his office. She knew what the look meant, a bad dream, a nightmare. He closed the door to his office and called up on his computer a map of the country. He heard a tentative knock on his door and invited Justine in. Before he could ask what, she wanted she blurted out, "You know these dreams never happened until that woman moved in next door to you. Maybe she is a witch and has cast a spell over you. Ever think of that?"

"She and her husband moved in almost two months before the dreams began. That was when I first met her. This is no time to begin talking about something that doesn't exist. This is the twenty-first century, there is no such things as witches, goblins or ghosts," he replied, and he thought about the symbol and what it possibly represented. No. There was no such thing as witches, a witch in his life.

"Maybe so, but just imagine that there are. What can you do about them? Nothing. That is why I said you should talk to Mary Ellen. See if she can help," Justine quickly replied.

He thought about what she said and answered, "What would Mary Ellen be able to do?"

"Just talk to her," Justine replied.

He let Justine go and put what she had said out of his mind. He returned to the map of the country and decided he would drive to San Antonio. He had eleven days before his appointment. It didn't seem that far, and it wouldn't be that difficult, after all he had already driven through San Antonio with Clare on their trip to Florida. The drive would get him away from the office for a while, would relax him and gave him time to think. Think about the dreams with no interruptions or work demands.

First thing to do was to let everyone know he would be gone for a while. He put it in a memo and sent it to all department heads. He called his two assistants into his office and told them he would be gone for a while, since they knew about his bad dreams, they accepted where he was going and why. It was not a big deal, but he would prefer that the two of them would keep it quiet. They should keep working on his company expansion plan and their new office. When he returned he hoped to read through their plan, make suggestions, changes and at the next board meeting present it. If something important came up, they had his cell number and could call him.

He let Justine go and asked Mary Ellen to wait. When they were alone, he said," Justine said I should talk to you about the nightmares I've been having, that maybe you can help, have an explanation."

"There is really nothing that I can do or say. I'm not sure why she said something like that to you," Mary Ellen replied. She would not look him in the eye.

Peter would not dismiss her but pressed on. "She was insistent that I talk to you, tell me why. What did you say to her that would cause her to have so great a concern?"

Mary Ellen fidgeted around and wouldn't look at Peter. He waited. She began. "You know I'm from Arkansas, the Ozarks area. Up in the Boston Mountains, in remote areas, there are some strange people. People who believe in the supernatural, curses, spells, and magic. I'm educated and know it's all bunk. Justine and I have talked about your dreams and…"

Mary Ellen stopped. She would not go on. Peter told her, "Finish what you had begun to say regardless of how ridiculous it may sound."

"The most popular of these strange people are the root doctors, hoodoos."

"Why are they called root doctors," he asked.

She was quiet for a moment and said, "Their power to cast a spell comes from the roots of plants, from herbs or berries. Most are not referred to as witches, but that is what they are. They prefer to be called root doctors or hoodoos. There are a lot of them. They are everywhere, not only in the mountains."

"So, I should be extra careful during the full moon?"

He didn't get a response from Mary Ellen. After a moment of silence, she said, "They do not meet at certain times of the month, during a full moon, special times of the year, special or historical dates, or some other times. They do not brew up a potion in a big cauldron, no bat wings, or eyes of lizards. There is no such thing as a black sabbath. Unlike in movies or on TV, they do not make sacrifices to the devil."

Again, Mary Ellen was silent for a moment. Peter just stared at her. Then her explanation came tumbling out. Once she started she hurried to tell Peter what she knew about root doctors and didn't wish to be interrupted. "They cannot contact the devil with a medium, control nature or animals such as a mouse, or insects. They cannot make objects, especially a person, levitate. They don't fly nor do they have a black cat that they use to communicate with the devil, unless it is a pet similar to what you or I would have. Some of them are religious. If you wish to refer to them as witches and not root doctors or hoodoos, religious ones would be white witches. They do not like to be thought of as witches because they do not consider the spells they cast as magic. There isn't one who is in charge, a head witch. Some are more powerful than others. No one knows why. Ask one how she became a witch, she will not be able to give you a good answer. One day she realized she had the gift, was one. The ones I knew always believed their supernatural powers were a gift. A gift from who or what could never be explained. Some don't know they are a witch. Most people think of witches as evil. They aren't. Most are benevolent. Forget what the bible says about them. They may cast a spell for a thousand different reasons for a person, love, health, luck, travel, intelligence, not to fear something in their life etcetera. They are of a non-evil nature. The most common is causing a person to love, cause a person to have good luck, a happy life and so on. They can't cause someone to die. Some may stray from being a white witch and cause a person to slip and fall, have headaches, a rash or whatever, but not die. Cast spells that will hurt you. A spell that could be considered evil. Maybe what you should avoid or shouldn't do and that would be it. They can't foretell the future. I've heard that very powerful witches can influence the weather, not cause it, or change it, but have it act in certain ways and they can communicate with each other. I don't know of anyone from back home that knew one of these powerful witches and I certainly don't know of one. It's just something I'd heard."

"How is one effecting me?"

"A witch or someone has called upon a witch to cast a spell on you, and she has. A spell to have bad dreams. The witch is the one calling to you in your dreams. Dreams that would affect, disrupt your everyday life."

Peter thought about what Mary Ellen said. After a moment he said, "You're right. This all sounds like bunk. I shouldn't have asked you. You can go, that is all," and he motioned for her to leave.

Mary Ellen's hand was on his doorknob when Peter asked, "Who is this witch? Who could she be? How can I recognize her?" He didn't believe in reincarnation and now he had a renewed interest in hoodoos, witches.

"You can't, you will not know. She will confess, admit what she has done if you question her directly. She would not be able to lie or deny you. You may have never seen her, talked to her, but someone else has, asked the witch for her help. Like I said, they are most often called upon to cast a love spell on someone and I told Justine it sounds like that is what has happened to you. Not love, but a spell that would upset your life. After your breakup with Clare have you found yourself attracted to another woman?" She saw Peter shake his head no as he thought about his past and searched for someone he was attracted to. Was he attracted to Donna? No. When he didn't answer, she continued. "Make you fall in love with her," Mary Ellen replied.

Peter thought about what she just said. He has not fallen in love with anyone since Clare. Did he love Clare? If he did, could he forget about her as quickly and as easily as he did? No. He hadn't even been attracted to a woman since he and Clare split. He hadn't even dated anyone unless he counted the three times he went out with Donna and the first time was only for coffee. They never got serious.

Why was he listening to Mary Ellen? Why was he paying her any attention? He thought about what she had said and shook his head in disbelief. When he did, he saw her rub the whatever hanging from her necklace. He asked, "Is that a root you've attached to your necklace? The one I gave you for Christmas last year?"

"A gift from an aunt. She got it from a root doctor. It is considered a talisman. Instead of a stone, jewel, or some man-made material it is from nature, a root. It is supposed to keep evil spirits away. I wear it to please my mother and her sister. It means nothing."

"Then why do you wear it?" Peter asked. "I've seen you rub it from time to time."

"It will protect me and my family," Mary Ellen replied. "I don't think about rubbing it, I just do." She was quiet for a moment and said, "My root is from a root doctor. I don't know what plant it is from and most likely never will. To make the spell work, the root would have to have a spell put on it and then be given to you to eat by the person who is after you. My mother made me bite a small piece of it and eat it last time I was home." She paused, "Justine has said that the dreams started about the time Jan, your new neighbor, moved in."

"She didn't just move in; it was a couple of months before the dreams began."

"Somehow, someway she has become smitten by you. She may not know it, but she may want you. She's a witch or she could have gone to a witch, wants you to be her soul mate, asked for a spell."

"But the spell would have had to be cast on me, to love her, want her. If she had a spell cast on me it is not working. I've known her for several months and as far as I know, I don't want or love her." The thought of her flashed through his mind, at least the love her part. He often wanted her, wanted her for sex. He did not have any feelings of love for her other than that.

"She will be patient. Patience is one thing that is known for sure about witches. She knows that deep down, someday you will be hers, wait days, months, or years. She may love you, want you but has to have you eat a root on which a spell has been cast and has been given to her by a witch, a spell so that you will fall in love with her, want her in return. Have you ever eaten anything that she has given you? Something that she has cooked? Maybe a pie, cookies? Ever given you anything to drink?"

Peter thought back over the seven months or so that he has known his neighbor Jannette. "I have never eaten or drunk anything she may have given me." Peter had told his analyst that he had in the past lusted after her. Again, he thought about his neighbor. Did he want her? Yes. But did he love her. No. Could it be why she suggested they have coffee some morning? No. Is it nonsense? Yes.

"As a neighbor, is it possible that somehow she has been able to break into your house and doctor food or drink?" Mary Ellen asked.

"I guess it is possible. I wouldn't know," and again he said, "I haven't fallen for her, love her."

"She may not be a witch but sent by one and Jan wouldn't know it," Mary Ellen said.

"But let's forget about her, if what you say is true, it could be any number of women I know. How about Donna the caterer?"

Mary Ellen said, "She would be a good possibility. You've definitely eaten something she prepared or put in your drink. The fact that you didn't meet her until well after the dreams started could easily be explained because she asked a witch to have her meet the man of her dreams, the man she needs. And that man is you. Donna was able to wait for months for you to come along."

"The big question, what does this have to do with the terrible nightmares I have been having?" Peter asked.

"I don't know how they would be tied together, unless…" and Mary Ellen didn't finish.

Peter had been caught up in what she had been saying and wanted to know. "Unless what?"

"You have helped or upset a more powerful witch and she won't let you sleep. It's not love at all. Neither your neighbor, Donna or another woman has had a spell cast on them or have asked for a spell to be cast on you," Mary Ellen finished. "The witch is calling to you. Only she can tell you why you have bad dreams. It could go back to when you were with Clare, she was a witch or the one who gave you something to eat or drink that had a root in it. The spell caused the dreams to happen. If it was Clare who has had a spell cast on you, I don't know what her aim is or was, except to make you unhappy. The deviousness of witches is very difficult to understand. How and why they do things can't be grasped. Please remember all this that I've told you is what I have been told by family and friends. I have no firsthand knowledge of any of it."

Peter thought back to when he was with Clare. The dreams began when they were still together. Was it possible that Clare knew the direction their relationship would take? That they would separate, and it is her way of punishing him. But she was the reason they broke up, it wasn't him. He had no inkling that she didn't like him, had another lover, lovers. And it didn't work, he was not unhappy. With the help of his analyst, he soon forgot about Clare. No. It was an impossibility what Mary Ellen told him. There were no such things as witches and spells.

After a moment Peter asked, "Are there men who are witches?"

"Most likely. They are referred to as wizards, but I've never known of one, back home they have always been women," was Mary Ellen's response.

He didn't give much thought to what he had just heard, and he had enough time to think about it. "Like I said, this is the twenty-first century, there were no such things as witches. May as well begin thinking about ghosts next. Thank you, Mary Ellen," and he let her go.

When he awoke the next morning, he wasn't in a panic. He wasn't cold or sweating. He believed and hoped the dreams were over. Could what he and Mary Ellen talked about cause his dreams to be resolved? No. There were no such things as witches, a spell cast upon him. Peter didn't know why he was having the dreams. The more he thought about them he believed he would he be able to accept them even though he couldn't stop them. He didn't know but he would try. Maybe the talk with Mary Ellen had helped.

That morning he looked forward to going to work. He dressed and was about to leave. When he opened his door, there was Jannette and she smiled at him. She had not moved. Peter had just not seen her. Jannette wore a puffy down coat to below her knees, almost to the furry pull-on boots that she wore and over what Peter believed was her bath robe. She held out his paper. The way the sun lit her from the rear, her blonde hair glowed. Had she had it done, he thought, or was she naturally blonde? He was dumb struck for a moment. He believed her to be an angel. Then the real word came crashing in when she asked, "I was about to ring your doorbell. I came over to ask if I could have your paper when you are through with it. My friend Marge called me and said there was an article in this morning's paper about my ex-husband."

"Yes. Keep it. I'll get one at work," he answered. He believed that she did in fact get a divorce since she referred to her spouse as her ex-husband. Would he attempt to go after her when he returned? Date her as his analyst suggested? Witch or not, would he try to get her in bed? No.

She thanked him, about to turn and head to her house when she asked, "Have you and Clare broken up? I haven't seen her for a while."

He was still in shock from seeing her and believing her to be an angel, but he regained his composure and said, "Yes. We have parted."

He remembered what Ms. Schwarz said about him lusting after her. It was true. He saw her naked for a moment in his mind under her puffy down coat. Could he perform with her? He didn't know but believed he would like to try and find out, but he knew he wouldn't. She again thanked him for his paper, turned around and headed to her house. If she was a witch, she didn't look like one. She didn't have a hook nose with a wart on it, no black pointed hat, no cackle when she talked. Where was her black cat? Wouldn't she have one? Witches always did. No, according to Mary Ellen. Then there was her necklace with a cross. Would a witch wear a cross? The cross she wore was always present. Like it was today. Could a witch be religious? Yes, according to Mary Ellen. He didn't know and wouldn't ask Mary Ellen if his neighbor was religious, could she be a witch. Why give her story more credence? But he did, think about witches, and spells. Had he fallen under Mary Ellen's, Mary Ellen's what? Spell. She had him thinking about the supernatural, witches and spells. And the symbol he often saw. The symbol of ancient devil worshippers. Why did he see it?

No black hair this morning but a warm smile from a, a what? He didn't know but it promised to be a good day. First no bad dream and then to see an angel. He didn't pay any attention to the fact that during the night it had snowed.

Most of the morning he sat in his office with the door closed. He began to search on his computer for witches and wizards and their history. He didn't believe in them nor did he believe in what Mary Ellen had said, but he was curious. For hours he read about their activities, covens, hexes, spells, and other forms of magic. They were surely believed to exist in the Middle Ages and were burned at the stake. The most famous of these was one that he casually knew about, the Salem witch hunts. He remembered seeing the play *The Crucible*. It was required watching in an English class he was in, but the only mention of a witch or what she looked like, was her name Abigale, accused of being one and that was by a jealous accuser who wanted Abigale's husband. But today their existence was superstition. He found that most of their activities took place during the full moon and especially around Halloween. The result of some imaginative businesses and fairy tale authors who mainly wanted to promote Halloween.

The blurbs he read took him to movies. Everything that a witch could do he realized was the imagination and resourcefulness of the movie business and its special effects department. And today with computer technology, anything was possible. The only thing holding a person back would be his or her imagination. The one movie that he had seen with a witch in it was *The Wizard of Oz.* But there were three, one good and two bad, one bad one was killed when Dorothy's house fell on her. But the second witch was good and she had blonde hair like his neighbor's. He needed to stop thinking of his neighbor as a witch, she couldn't be because they didn't exist. The third was a bad witch if he remembered correctly, was stereotypical, big nose, green, with a pointed hat and did she have a broom? He couldn't remember. Then he remembered that as a child he had read *Hansel and Gretel.* It had been illustrated but he knew the author and artist had made up what she looked like. He vaguely remembered what the witch looked like and at the time she frightened him, or was what she was about to do to the two children?

The more he looked the more skeptical he became. There was nothing in real life as a witch and there wasn't one in his life.

When he got home that evening, on his doorstep was his newspaper with a note that thanked him. Inside he opened the paper and found a section had been cut out. He didn't remember what had been there and had no interest in finding out.

That evening he continued to return to what Mary Ellen had said to him about a spell cast on him. Was it possible? A grain of truth in what Mary Ellen said? No. This was the twenty first century, no such things as witches and spells. The more he tried to forget about what Mary Ellen had said, the more it came back and crept into his mind.

Chapter 6

Peter had more than a week before he needed to be in San Antonio. He was unable to put what Mary Ellen had told him out of his mind. Could it be true? A spell? No, impossible. But then as an afterthought he wondered, did such a person, a witch advertise? Before he went to bed, Peter absently minded began to look in the yellow pages for one. He found none listed.

Had Peter begun to give credence to what Mary Ellen had told him? There was no such thing as a witch. But why not give it a try, someone who cast spells was what he needed. Not very successful he went from the yellow pages to his computer. He opened sites that took him to sites of astrology, spiritual healers, mediums, wizards, and other references of the occult. Most revolved around fortune tellers and psychic readings. One common area of help was love. They could help you find love, bring a lost lover back or the other common area was money. They could help you be successful or give you lucky numbers. Some used roots or herbs. There was reference to magic, the mystical, white magic and spells cast. Many had an 800-telephone number to call. He opened several and was informed that the first call was free or for a mere five-ninety-five up to twenty-nine-ninety-five, his wishes could be granted, no direct contact was needed. Answer a few questions about his personal life, his birthday, age, and a credit card number were all that was needed. All that he would need to do was tell what he wanted done. Talk to a seer, and the call would only cost him three dollars a minute. The more sites he looked at the less believable they became. One guaranteed he could talk to a departed loved one or ancestors.

He scrolled through the sites that would take him to additional sites. A telephone number that caught his eye had a three-number prefix for the Denver area, not an 800 number. He double checked it with his yellow pages and there it was. The three-number prefix was for Denver. The site gave him more information of what could be provided. It said if he was having a problem in his life, he should contact this medium/psychic. He wouldn't need to tell her his problem, she would tell him what was troubling him and help. Guaranteed. She dealt with spirits, roots, palm reading and cards. Roots? Could she be a witch that Mary Ellen had referred to? To give the medium, not a witch, root doctor or hoodoo, more legitimacy the medium referred to herself as a Doctor.

Peter gave up on such a search was about ready to close his computer when he looked for spells. He found it only gave him definitions of the word. He continued to search and typed on his computer magical spells. This took him to a new and large number witches, astrologers, spiritual healers, wizards, mediums, and the like. Maybe not thousands of different spells but there seemed to be hundreds and a lot had a specific name of spells. Peter soon became tired of reading through the assortment of spells just as he became tired looking at different types of people who would cast them. He was about to close when he went back his computer and returned to the telephone number in Denver. It was only ten o'clock, but he was not ready to turn in. He might dream. He would watch TV for a while. Ten minutes later he was on the phone to Doctor Yolanda and made an appointment to visit her. She did not see people during the day, only saw customers at night. Peter arranged to see her. She would expect to see him tomorrow evening. He asked if Yolanda was her first or last name and was informed by her that it was her name period.

The next day he was glad he didn't have a bad dream. He went through the motions of work. What would Ms. Schwarz say to his meeting with a medium? Why not? She was the one who put the idea of someone from his past trying to contact him. Too late to think about what his analyst would say. He had made up his mind. He was desperate and would see it through. His analyst couldn't help. Could a medium/psychic? He knew he didn't believe in them, but he would give one a try. Once the seed had been planted, in the back of his mind, it had begun to grow, would grow and guide his life choices.

It was just getting dark that day as he drove to a part of Denver he was not familiar with, but with his car's GPS he found the doctor's address, and it was a house, an old house. His first thought when he saw it was it looked like something out of a movie, a house where teens went and be led into a supernatural occult horror journey. The house was not falling down but was in a state of disarray and needed to have a fresh coat of paint.

At the door he rang the bell. The door was opened by a middle age woman he believed was, was of what heritage? She was dark skinned, but he couldn't peg her into any ethnic group. She was not dressed like the mediums he had seen in movies or on TV. He could smell cigarette smoke, was it from her or was it the house, her yellow teeth told him she possibly was a smoker. She was average height and weight, wore a simple dress and her graying hair was tightly pulled back and tied. She wore one earing, a large round circle in her right ear. After he introduced himself, Doctor Yolinda took his hand and led him into her living room, neither spoke. The room's curtains were drawn and in the dimly lit room she lit two candles that were on the table where he sat. She sat opposite him and asked if he wanted her to read his palm or read her cards. "Why would you want to do either?" he asked. She didn't answer. After a moment he added, "I'd like to try roots."

Doctor Yolinda at his request was quick to answer, "I don't do them anymore, they were too unreliable. Besides, it is winter. Cards and your palm are more useful, trustful. I will do either to discover why you are here and how I can help you," she answered.

Peter was not too keen on her touching him, so he decided on the cards. He watched her as she spread the cards on the table, face down and began to wash them. He recognized the cards as tarot before she placed them on the table. She swirled them around and asked Peter to tell her when to stop. From the light of the candles, he could see the yellow on her index and middle finger as she swished the cards around, he thought the tell-tale result of a heavy smoker. When he finally told her to stop, she gathered the cards into a neat pile and began to turn them over, one at a time. After she turned over the first card she began to tell Peter why he was there. It was a statement as well as a question, "Money problems."

Peter looked at the card and the face of the tarot card told him nothing, all that he could do was shake his head no. She muttered some nonsense and said the next card would tell her if she was wrong. Before she turned over the card she attempted to engage Peter in small talk about his life, his job, his hobbies. Was he married? Did he have children? To all her small talk he remained silent. He would not give her a clue to why he had come to see her. Her job was to tell him and help.

She turned the next card, "Tell me about your romance problems."

Again, he shook his head "No. Don't have any."

A flip of a third card, "You have thought of contacting a departed one?"

"No."

A health problem was next, and it was followed by additional tries, guesses, to the reason why he was there. Unsuccessful as to why he wanted to see her, she drifted away from trying to guess Peter's problem and went off on a tangent and began to tell him of his future. He realized that Doctor Yolanda was not a medium, a witch who could help him. He told her she was not very good since she couldn't identify his problem. "If you don't know why I need your help, how you can help me?"

She tried to excuse herself, "You are hard to read, so unless I know what your problem is it is impossible to help you." He concluded that his first inclination that there was no such thing as witches and spells was the correct one. Yolanda could not help him. He got up from the table, threw a twenty at her, "For your trouble," and made his way to her door. She didn't follow him or say anything.

Chapter 7

That night he again dreamed about fishing, not at Wild Bear Creek, but at Shay's Run. He drove to the small stream and then he saw its sign, routed into a cross timber mounted to a post that had been secured into the ground. To the left the stream was too small to fish and most of the water had been diverted underground or was covered over with fallen tree branches and brush. He began walking down stream and after he walked several hundred yards the run had had several springs empty into it and the water became deeper and fishable. And so, he began to fish. He was able to see the fish in the open pools and saw them scatter when they caught sight of him. He continued and would do so until the stream reached the large lake it emptied into. The further he walked the fewer trees he saw, and they soon became dead as the stream spread out and took on a green color, the water wasn't green, but duck weed began to cover its surface.

Peter didn't remember this drab, barren landscape from before nor the duck weed. All that he could see was the green duck weed and dead trees. He never remembered seeing it before. He realized he couldn't move. His fishing boots had become mired in mud. The green had disappeared. He struggled to free himself and only succeeded in sinking deeper into the muck. He became desperate. He had to free himself, but how? He tried to use his fishing rod as a pole and he tried to pull himself free, but the mud kept pulling him deeper. As he twisted and turned, he saw bubbles rise to the top of the mud. He believed he could smell the mud. He could reach into a boot and unfasten the inner part where it was secured to his calf. Peter could feel his foot become free of his fishing boot and he was able to pull it free. Then he unfastened the other boot, pull his leg out of the boot and he was out of the mud, lying on top of it. Peter would try to use his fishing rod as a paddle. But he didn't have it. He tried to crawl on top of the mud, spitting it out when it got into his mouth. Was it going to choke him? More and more made its way into his mouth. He spat and coughed. Was he going to be able to reach solid ground, the shore, get out of this muck? That was when he felt something hold him back and his head sank into the mud.

He coughed loud and spit out the mud and that was when he awoke. He bolted up on his bed. He was shaking, wet and covered with mud. How could it have happened? Where did the mud come from? Ms. Schwarz suggestion that he somehow had it happen before he went to sleep was an impossibility. Where would he find mud in January in snow covered Denver? He tried to keep calm then stumbled to the bathroom and cleaned up. The next day at seven o'clock he was at his analyst's door. She had no explanation for his latest dream except that his latest dreams centered around water.

His analyst was able to calm him down and he returned to work. The first thing Peter needed to do was settle a dispute between distribution and sales. With his two assistants, his boss, and the heads of the two departments it required all morning to settle. After lunch he decided to spend serious time and look at the first draft, the outline his two assistants had formulated to his idea of a new expansion. He had to steer himself away from his nightmare. When asked about their plan, his response had always been that he was looking at it. He decided that they were on the right track and told them to continue. Justine left his office, but Mary Ellen stayed behind.

When they were alone, she said, "I hope that what I told you several days ago about root doctors and casting spells didn't upset you. It was me just spouting off."

"No, it didn't upset me. It was interesting hearing you talk about it, but I didn't put place credence in what you said."

Mary Ellen turned to leave when Peter asked, "If I wanted to talk to one of your root doctors, how would I go about it. I'm sure a root doctor, or witch, is not listed in the yellow pages."

She stopped. "I agree with you. You might find either on the internet, but they are not for real. A real root doctor would never advertise. We know about them through word of mouth."

"Are there any in Denver?" he asked her.

Mary Ellen hesitated for a moment. She should not ever have brought up the idea of spells and witches. Her supervisor has taken an interest in what she had told him. "Not that I know of," was her reply.

She was again prepared to leave Peter's office when he followed up with, "How about the state of Colorado? Up in the mountains? We have a lot here in the state."

Again, Mary Ellen answered him with, "Not that I know of." It ended their conversation.

Near the end of the day Peter was getting ready to leave when Mary Ellen knocked lightly on his door. "I called back home and asked mom if she knew of a root doctor in Denver or Colorado. She said she would ask around and get back to me. She just called. There is one in Boulder and gave me her name and address." She handed Peter a slip of paper with the information on it. "I wouldn't put much stock in what I told you. I think it's a lot of bunk. But if you are interested, wish to pursue it, I guess I can't stop you."

Peter took the slip of paper, glanced at it, folded it and put it in his pocket. If Mary Ellen believed that it was hard to believe in what she had told him, maybe he shouldn't believe what she said. There had to be a real and logical reason for the dreams, not a spell that had been cast. He thanked her.

That night he decided to begin packing for his trip to San Antonio. When he was getting undressed for bed the slip of paper Mary Ellen had given him fell out of his shirt pocket. He looked at it and saw the name Zetta Mae Hassing and her address. He didn't remember seeing her address the first time he looked at the name on the piece of paper. He paid it no mind, crumbled the piece of paper and threw it in a waste basket.

That night he was walking through a growth of trees and there it was, the symbol carved into a tree. He saw the light glimmer and moved toward it. The silent plea called to him and he struggled to reach it. The harder he struggled, the more difficult it was for him to move. Then suddenly he was sliding down a steep embankment. Then he saw a roiling river below him. He was going to fall into it. This time he didn't feel that the woman needed him, but he heard her say she needed his help. He believed he heard himself say he was coming. He grabbed for bushes that slipped by him. He was able to grab hold of one just to have it slip through his hand and he had a handful of leaves. He reached out again and felt the branches of a bush just as his legs reached the water. He struggled to pull himself up from the water. Could the churning water pull him in? Could he drown? The fall and the water terrified him. As he looked out over the water he saw two eyes at the water level looking back at him. He believed they were eyes, reminded him of eyes. He was not sure. They seemed to be moving toward him. He kicked at the water and his feet found solid ground, the shoreline. He felt himself shaking as he pushed with his feet and he struggled. He reached out and his hand encountered another small bush. He was able to grab hold of it. He had to get back up the hill and pushing and pulling he began to crawl. At the top of the hill was his woman. He could feel her call to him, she needed him. Get away from the eyes. Could he make it to the top, could he reach her, help her?

He awoke in a sweat. Peter was shaking and his legs were wet. How did this happen? How did what he dreamed become real? He would meet with Ms. Schwarz that afternoon, tell her of his latest dream. Could she prescribe something stronger than the Xanax? He would buy some marijuana and try it before sleep. Would it help? He didn't know. What he did know was the sleeping pills she had suggested had not done the job and he had stopped taking them.

He had gotten up and dressed and skipped breakfast. Ready to go to work he first looked out, through the window in his door. The last person he wished to run into was his neighbor. Did he believe what Mary Ellen had told him? Could she be a witch? No. But why take a chance. He got to his car quickly and drove to his workplace. When he met his two assistants they were both aware that he had a bad dream last night. They could see the look on his face. He entered his office and sat. He needed to get busy, so he began to read company reports. A knock on his door interrupted him and he looked up and said, "Yes?"

Justine asked, "Can I get you anything?" She waited but he didn't answer her. "Can I help?"

After a moment he told her, "No. I'll be alright. On second thought a cup of coffee, black, would be nice."

Justine left and ten minutes later she returned with the coffee. She gave it to Peter and was aware that he did not wish to talk. She didn't say anything, turned and left his office.

As usual he left early for lunch. He sat in the diner and Maxie served him. Neither said anything more than what he ordered. When she served him, she commented that it looked like winter had finally arrived. When it was time for his appointment he went to his analyst's office. She had nothing to add to how she had been helping him. Talking and understanding had to suffice. She was still convinced that there had been something in his past that was manifesting itself through his dreams. Something that he had repressed and was maybe so terrible that he was able to not remember it even through hypnosis. Was he ready to meet with the dream specialist, the drive to Texas? Maybe the specialist would be able to uncover it. She wrote him a prescription for Valium. Maybe the two drugs would be a help.

He left Ms. Schwarz's office and headed for the elevator. He had the Valium prescription in his hand and decided to put it into his wallet until he was able to get to the drugstore. When he opened his wallet he saw a crumpled piece of paper that had been folded and placed in the bill-fold area. He took it out and unfolded it. It was the slip of paper that Mary Ellen had given him. He remembered throwing it away, or did he? How did it get into his wallet? He didn't remember but assumed that at some time he retrieved the piece of paper and put it into his wallet. He didn't want to believe that he imagined he had thrown it away. Was he beginning to become forgetful? His nightmares were beginning to seriously affect his life.

What Mary Ellen had said to him kept gnawing at him, but he was sure that what she had said could not be true. He would not follow up on what she said, would not try to contact the root doctor who lived in Boulder. Peter crumbled up the slip of paper a second time. He would depend on his visit to the dream specialist to help him solve his problem.

Later that day it was late afternoon, and he was in Boulder. He thanked whoever invented it, his GPS, because it instructed him to go northwest from Boulder to find the address. Peter may have gone to college in Boulder, but he was not familiar with the outlying areas. He drove on a secondary road away from the downtown area. A left from the road turned into single one lane that had been plowed only wide enough for one vehicle. He saw the numbers on the mailboxes as he passed them. He was looking for 1161. He came to 1157 and he slowed down. The next box did not have a number on it, so he kept driving until he saw 1167. He had passed Zetta Mae's house. He was able to turn around and drove to the unnumbered mailbox and drove into the driveway. The house was a single-story brick with shrubbery around it, bare twigs now poking through the snow. In the yard he saw three children trying to make a snowman. They saw an unknown person drive into their driveway so all three approached Peter's car. He put his window down and told them he was looking for Zetta Mae Hassing. The oldest, a boy, replied, "My mom's Zetta Mae but our last name is Gallo". Peter had no idea how long ago Zetta Mae had last lived in Arkansas but assumed she was the correct person to see. He opened his door and got out.

Addressing the boy who answered him he asked, "Would you tell your mom that I'm here and would like to see her?"

The boy ran to the house and went inside. The remaining two, who he guessed were girls because they were so bundled up, stared at him. After a moment the boy came out of the house and he saw a thin woman holding a baby standing in the doorway. He walked to her, introduced himself and told her he needed to talk to her. She invited him into the house and told her son to go play. She pointed to the table in the living room, told him to take off his coat and sit. She sat across from him and Peter saw a woman probably in her mid-thirties, stringy long light brown hair and looked frumpy in her house clothes. She asked, "What can I do for you Mr. Frost?"

No sense in beating around the bush. "Zetta Mae, I need a spell."

For a moment she looked at him in astonishment and didn't say anything. He repeated his request. She angrily asked, "Who told you about me!? Told you I could cast a spell for you!? Who!?" she demanded.

Peter could sense the anger in her voice. Did he make a mistake? He didn't want to get Mary Ellen in trouble. "A friend, back in the Boston Mountains," was his response.

Both were quiet for a moment. It was obvious that this man who came to visit her knew who and what she was. She seemed to have settled down when she told Peter, "I gave up all the magic, spell stuff, the practice of a root doctor. My husband knows nothing of my past and I want to keep it that way."

Peter waited a moment and explained what and why he needed a spell.

To his request she replied, "I cannot do it. I do not believe I can make your bad dreams cease. If they were the product of another witch's curse, that witch, root doctor would have to free you."

He persisted, would not let go of the reason he came to see her. "Please, help me," he pleaded.

"There's nothing for me to do, can do."

Again, as earnestly as possible, he pleaded, "Try." He was now convinced that what Mary Ellen had told him was true. There was such a thing as a root doctor, a good witch. She could cast a spell and relive him of his malady.

"The one who cast the spell is the only one who will be able to remove it." After a moment Zetta Mae got up from the table, "Stay here," she said. She placed the baby that she had been holding in its crib.

He watched her go to a cupboard and pick up a plastic herb jar. What was it? He didn't know. Peter watched as she sprinkled some into her open hand. She spat on it and began to roll it around between her two palms. She closed her eyes, mumbled something, spat on it a second time and continued to roll it. After a moment she stopped, opened her eyes pulled a paper towel from a roll at the sink, dropped the rolled-up herb onto it and wrapped the paper towel around it. She handed it to him. "Tonight, before you go to sleep, put it into a pot of water and boil it. Do not strain the herb. When it is cool enough, drink half of it. In your mind tell yourself what you want to have happen, then drink the remainder. That's all I can think of. I doubt it will do any good, like I said only the witch who cursed you can relive you from the curse. Do not come back."

"What will you tell your husband when he asks about me?"

"You were trying to sell me insurance."

Peter thanked her, got in his car and returned to Denver. That night he followed Zetta Mae's instructions. He hoped her spell would work.

He was in a bad snowstorm. He had difficulty trying to move and the snow was getting deeper. He fell, struggled to rise, and continued toward the warm glow. He was cold, wore only a short sleeve tee-shirt, summer shorts and his feet were bare. He knew he had to reach the glow and the woman who needed him. The glow would warm him and he would be able to help her. He felt it was getting colder and he was going to freeze to death, die in the snow. He fell and his mouth filled with snow. He shivered and began to cough.

Peter woke coughing and he was cold. He was shaking and when he looked at his feet he saw that they were red, red from the cold snow. How could that be!? He was on his bed, covered with a sheet and blanket. His first thought was that the heat was off. He pushed himself off the bed and the room was warm. How could it have happened? He stumbled to the bathroom and stood under a hot shower until he could feel the cold leave. He thought about his visit to Zetta Mae's and what she had told him. Did he believe her? Yes. Her spell didn't work, wouldn't work. If he believed what Mary Ellen had said about being cursed, and he began to believe what Zetta Mae had said, how could he find the witch who cursed him? He couldn't. Didn't know who she could be, how to find her. Who were the women in his recent life? Clare, but she was gone. Could he ask her, or would she hang up as soon as she knew it was him? Jannette was a possibility, but he only thought of her in a carnal way, and not even that lately. But someday, somehow he would ask her if she cursed him. He was the reason that he and Donna never made it beyond the first several dates. It could be her. If she were the one, his dream woman would not have interfered. Who else? There was Maxie in the restaurant. No. She never gave him a hint that she thought him attractive. Same for the company's receptionist. No. She was happily engaged. These were the only women he had contact with besides his analyst and assistants. All three he dismissed. He had been keeping away from single women, especially at work. He had begun to believe in what Mary Ellen had said to him. There could not be witches in this day and age especially in his life. Peter had to stop believing in what Mary Ellen had told him. But could he?

There was no help for him. Ms. Schwarz wouldn't believe him, that he believed in such baloney. She would ask how an educated man like him could believe in such nonsense. And it was nonsense, witches, and curses. He had to forget about the supernatural. His hope was that the sleep clinic could be a help, would be a help.

Later that day his session with his analyst got them nowhere. She could not believe that Peter's dreams were manifesting the dreams in his real life. He had to somehow gotten wet before he went to sleep, or a better explanation, Peter was sleep walking. Both scenarios he believed were untrue, he had done neither.

Chapter 8

With a half dozen books on disc, Peter took a lazy two-day drive to San Antonio. He focused on driving and at the end of the day he was tired and slept. No pleas for help. Maybe the secret to no bad dreams was to be very tired before he went to bed. He never told Ms. Schwarz about his foray with an afterlife group, a medium/psychic, and a root doctor/witch. He would put all behind him and begin to believe in reality, the twenty first century. He had made special arrangements with the lawn and tree service to keep his place snow free and Justine to check on his home occasionally and his mail all forwarded to his office address. He stopped his newspaper. The GPS in his car was a big help. He did not need to look at a map or ask anyone for directions. Here was the sleep research clinic. He parked and called Dr. Wesbaumh. Peter was instructed where he should meet with the team of sleep researchers. No dreams or pleas for help that night and the following day he drove to the research facilities. It was a modern looking building connected to one of the city's universities. He was greeted upon admittance to the building by first giving his insurance card that was scanned and copied. How much, if any, of this would be covered, he didn't know. That was followed with a half dozen forms to fill out that described his medical history, his psychological history, and any medication he was taking. Did he smoke, drink and how much, do drugs. Many of the questions on this form he was not able to answer but he did the best that he could. He was asked about his parents, friends, both male and female, games that he played, organizations that he belonged to, what type of person he thought himself to be. There were a series of questions that asked what he would do in a particular situation. Then he was told to wait.

It was well over half an hour before he was invited by a woman, he thought was a nurse, into her office. It turned out that she was one of the researchers and introduced herself as Dr. Spiltz. She was going to do a psychological work up on him. The first thing she suggested was that he stop taking any prescription drugs, the Xanax and Valium. An hour or more of questions concerning his life. At first the questions centered on his sleep habits. Did he sleep regularly and for how long on average each night? Did he eat or drink anything before he slept? Did he have trouble falling asleep, and how many times during the night did he awake? Soon the questions switched to his job, romances, joys in life as well as fears. She asked several, what he thought of as, personal questions concerning his sex life. Peter hadn't had sex since Clare and he separated, over seven months now. Except for the fact that he was having bad dreams, which were affecting his daily life, he wasn't asked to describe them except for the fact that he found himself in a perilous situation and would wake up in a panic. Done with the questions he was to undergo a brain scan. Tomorrow, he was told, he would meet Dr. Wesbaumh and the doctor would clarify what they were going to do. He was to show up early, wear comfortable clothes. He should stay awake if possible tonight so that he could sleep tomorrow in their lab. First Dr. Wesbaumh would interview him and it was possible that Peter would be asked to try and sleep. It would be in the afternoon, but he thought that he would be able to do it or at least try.

He was assigned living quarters attached to the clinic so that he could be monitored. He was to treat it as a hotel room. He could relax, watch TV, come, and go as he pleased. He could eat out but the clinic, and the hospital it was attached to, had a good cafeteria and its prices were reasonable. It opened at 6 am and stayed open until 9 pm. Again, no pleas for help that night, but he had a strong feeling of thanks for coming. Was the dream clinic going to be an answer to his bad dreams? He felt good and that he had made the correct decision about attending.

The next morning he met the good doctor, a man of about fifty, hair turning gray and prematurely going bald who liked to wear glasses that were always low on his nose so that he had to look over them. He asked more detailed questions about Peter's dreams, all the while taking notes. "Dr. Schwarz sent me an overview of her work with you. I'm fascinated by the fact that one dream runs into another, picks up were one ended. Is it possible that you only imagine that the dreams were a continuation of the previous one?" the doctor asked.

"No," Peter replied. "Something that I saw in a previous dream while I was walking or running, I saw again, or something that I was doing in my last dream, I continued to do. It picked up where the previous one ended."

"And the woman has long black hair and green eyes, but you've never seen her. Is that correct?" Dr. Wesbaumh asked.

"Yes."

"How did you know what she looked like?" was the next thing the doctor wanted to know.

"I don't know. I just do," was Peter's reply.

"Could you have seen her in an earlier dream and forgot," was the next question asked.

Peter thought about what he had been asked and eventually said, "No. I don't remember ever having seen her in real life or a dream."

"And the dreams are affecting your awake life. For instance, when you wished to make love to a current girlfriend, Donna. The dream came to you?" Dr. Wesbaumh asked.

"It wasn't a dream, I, I, just couldn't perform, get an erection. I heard the woman in my dreams, her desperate silent plea for help. It killed the moment."

"What did Donna say to your explanation?" was the doctor's next question.

Peter hesitated before he answered, "I didn't explain or make an excuse. I took her home and never saw her again."

"Have you been with another woman since?" he asked.

"No," was Peter's answer. "No women since Clare and I separated almost six, seven months ago." The same answer he gave to Ms. Spiltz.

Dr. Wesbaumh was silent for a moment and then asked, "Tell me about who is trying to stop you. Is it a man?"

Peter didn't know and told the doctor. "I don't know who or what it is. I only assumed it was a him. Like the woman, I never clearly saw It or Him."

"Then how did you know it was trying to stop you?"

"I felt it, like I felt the woman calling to me. I didn't need to see it to feel its presence." More questions and answers followed. The interviews with Dr. Wesbaumh became a rehash of his work with Ms. Schwarz, but he focused more on Peter's sex life. The doctor returned to Peter's experience with Donna to no good result. The fact that he lusted after the, maybe, witch who lived next door, never came up. Peter became dissatisfied with the direction the interview was going. Eventually the interview ended and Peter was told that his dreams would be monitored and would start tomorrow. Not today. He should show up at noon and had been asked if he brought pajamas with him. Ms. Schwarz had suggested them, and he was glad he listened to her.

While at the clinic Peter did not have bad dreams nor did he feel the pleas for help. For the rest of the week Peter would have several electrodes attached to his head or a mask over his head and he slept. His thoughts and dreams were recorded and studied. He didn't remember most of what he dreamed but the doctor, Ms. Phelps, said there was nothing unusual about his sleep and dream pattern. She was also a doctor and always dressed in a white lab coat. Peter never saw Dr. Spiltz again. He didn't know if Dr. Phelps or Dr. Spiltz were shapely because the coats masked their bodies. He believed both to be pretty but didn't imagine having sex with them. After the first interview with Dr. Wesbaumh, he did not see the doctor again but had been handed off to his assistant, Dr. Phelps. He did have two dreams concerning his unseen woman, but all she did was to plead for his help. There was no evil being who tried to stop him. He was never put in a situation that he thought was life threatening. The scan of his brain did not detect any abnormalities.

At the end of the first week Peter concluded that his sleep was the focus of clinic, not his dreams. He slept in the afternoons into the evening, which was a question to him, why not at night? He would get up, dress, and make it to the cafeteria in time to have a late dinner. He would be placed in a darkened room, on a comfortable bed with pleasant music in the background. Several electrodes would be attached to his head and he was encouraged to sleep. He told Dr. Phelps about his dreams and she listened but gave him no advice or possible explanations. She asked him several questions about his past, women in his past who could be a possible clue to his dreams. Dr. Phelps could read Ms. Schwarz's documentation of his meetings with his analyst and get the answers to her questions. To Peter the sleep sessions and follow-up were a repeat of what he had done with his analyst, a continuation, like his dreams.

During his second week he met a graduate student, a woman sleeper. She was a student from the university who was a sleeping subject and being paid by the sleep clinic to have her dreaming monitored. She was short, a little overweight, pretty but what stood out about her was that for her size she had big breasts. It was a wonder that they didn't pull her over. He was sure that the imbalance they caused surely hurt her back. He thought about what she would look like with no clothes on. It was difficult for him to imagine because he had never seen a naked woman this small with breasts that large. Would he like to find out? Yes. Would he? No. He was eating his dinner in the cafeteria when she asked if she could join him. He pushed out a seat for her and she sat. They began talking. "My name is Cindy. I believe that I've seen you in the sleep clinic. What are you here for?" she asked as soon as she sat down. She took a bite of her sandwich.

"Nice to meet you Cindy, I'm Peter. I have bad dreams, nightmares that cause me to have panic attacks. The good doctor is going to try and find out why and hopeful be able to make them stop. And you?"

"The clinic is studying me. For what I don't know. I can go to classes in the morning, sleep in the afternoons and have nights to study. Since my biological time clock is messed up, I will, can sleep in the afternoon make up for staying awake at night. I've been told I'm over sexed and they want to find out why and how it affects my life, romance. Do I dream about sex? How often? Do my dreams make me want to have sex as soon as I awaken? Etcetera, etcetera. I think it's a lot of bull, but it pays good and is putting me through school." Both were quiet for a while as they continued to eat. Why was she telling him this? He hardly knew her, and she was telling him something personal about her life. Her next statement caught him off base. "Would you like to sleep with me, have sex?" Peter was not sure how he should answer. After a moment of silence, she continued, "The clinic could monitor us, before, during and after. I wouldn't mind if you wouldn't."

Peter thought about what she asked and didn't respond, and another moment passed. He thought yes and quickly thought about a condom. Did he have one? No. Could he get one? Yes, and he would see her enormous breasts, but Peter knew he would not be able to perform with others watching him. He may have thought yes, but said, "No." He was not into casual sex and he wondered why she was so forward. Did Dr. Wesbaumh or Dr. Phelps set this up. Did either one of them wish to see how he would respond to a woman, to sex?

Both were quiet for a moment before Cindy casually said, "Think about it. Let me know."

Peter did think about it and he knew. "I don't know you, but I'll eat with you, talk with you, be friends with you but, I will not sleep with you." She looked disappointed but seemed to accept what he told her. They finished eating and parted.

He saw her several times in the cafeteria with different men. Neither of the two ever connected again. Either she was not pleased he would not sleep with her, or the good doctors called her off if Peter would not have sex with her. What would, could having sex with a stranger have to do with his dreams? It made no sense. Maybe it was to study her, or was it to study him? How would he respond to a woman, sex? Did the clinic wish to find out? Would she or another woman be part of their research of his nightmares? Peter didn't believe so. He soon dismissed the idea.

After one sleep session Dr. Phelps said he had an exceptionally good reading. "Can you remember what you dreamed about?"

Peter slowly shook his head no and tried to remember what he had dreamed about. What was a good reading he wondered? The doctor tried to have Peter relax right before he was to sleep and think about the unseen woman in his dreams. It worked to some degree. He didn't hear her but felt she was never in danger. He did not try to reach her. At the end of the second week the researchers could find no unusual brain activity. Peter didn't have any bad dreams, dreams that caused him to have a panic attack. For the next week his sleep in the afternoons was changed to sleep at night and then returned to the afternoon sessions. Ms. Phelps tried to check Peter's brain activity when he slept at night. Nothing. He was at a loss as to what to do next.

The sleep/dream clinic could not help him. After three weeks and no positive results, he decided to return to Denver. There seemed to be some doubt in Dr. Wesbaumh's analysis when Ms. Phelps consulted with him concerning Peter's dreams. Had he really been having bad dreams? Could it be that Peter was imagining that the dreams had really occurred? Had he gotten up and did to himself what he had dreamed and then fallen back to sleep. If he did, he wouldn't remember, but it would explain his post dreams where he was hurt, bleeding, muddy, wet. Did he walk in his sleep? Not to his knowledge and the clinic's research found no evidence that he did. Dr. Phelps wanted Peter to stay at the clinic for an additional month so that he could continue to be studied. Peter had serious reservations as to how effective the good doctor and his staff were. He did not believe that he was being helped or could be helped. He realized that the dream research had evolved into analysis. What could Dr. Wesbaumh and Dr. Phelps find that Ms. Schwarz couldn't? He lost all confidence in the research clinic, maybe it was trying to find out if sleep in the afternoon could make up for lost sleep at night as Cindy had explained. Peter made the decision to leave. They had not helped him. The only good thing that happened, he didn't have any bad dreams that caused a panic attack while he was there while being monitored.

On the day he was to leave it was cloudy and he thought chilly. He thanked the doctors for their trying and when he was leaving, he saw the woman who checked him in. "Have a safe trip home Mr. Frost," she said. "Sorry it's so dreary out and overcast. Right before you arrived we were having a continuation of summer, a warm spell during winter."

"Well, we can't do anything about the weather," he told her.

"No, but I bet it's sunny and warm in Florida," she said with a warm smile.

Peter waved an acknowledgement as he headed through the door. He had not paid much attention to her when he checked in and she was sitting behind her desk but now he was more conscious of her. He believed she was cute and the top of her, from the chair up, showed that she was well built. He thought about sex with her. Would he? No. Besides, he was leaving. Why hadn't the doctor, or doctors, have her proposition him instead of Cindy. Would he have taken her up on sex? Peter thought yes but he knew he would have said no.

He hadn't brought a lot of clothes with him so packing his one suitcase to leave took no time at all. When he had everything and was about to head out the door he thought about what Mary Ellen had said about a spell being cast on him. And here was this check-in person, now ready to check him out and talked about spells and casting them. Well not really, but the words came up in the same statement. In the back of his mind, he had to ask himself, was it possible that his life was being affected by a witch? Why had she mentioned Florida? The last and only time he had been there was last year with Clare. When he thought back on it, he came to the realization that his dreams began after his trip to Florida. Did some event there become the reason fo the dreams? He couldn't think of anything, but he remembered the moment that Clare had gotten into an argument, disagreement, with a fortune teller on the beach. Peter could hardly remember the woman, but he did recall that she said she would cast a spell on Clare. He didn't remember exactly what was said. Could there be a grain of truth in what Mary Ellen had said and the woman on the beach was truly a witch? No. He was an educated man and his experiences with reincarnation, Yolanda and Zetta Mae caused him to be sure that he didn't believe any of the supposed magic that people used. Fortune telling? No way. Even if it were true, how could a fortune teller cast a magic spell and on him. He never even talked to the woman. Better to forget all about it, the woman and Florida and head back home.

He put the idea of a witch out of his mind. The explanation that Mary Ellen had given him continued to resurface and he tried to quell it. He would not allow it to dominate his thoughts and worse, influence his actions. He headed to his car. Besides, it was already the middle of February and would be spring soon. He could go fishing. Real fishing, not dreaming about it. The thought of fishing made him more determined than ever to return to Denver. And his dreams, the anxiety medication that Ms. Schwarz had prescribed would have to suffice.

Chapter 9

It was a nice drive and as the receptionist said, it was warmer. His car's GPS took him where he wanted to go. There was the sign. He remembered it from before. Naples was the next exit to the right. He turned off the interstate and drove to the hotel, the second time he would stay there. Clare wanted to go to Naples because it reminded her of Italy, a country she had never been to and most likely would never go to. Did Naples, Florida, look anything like Naples, Italy? Most likely not. At the time, in the back of Peter's mind when Clare made the statement, he began planning their honeymoon to be in Italy. It would be a big surprise to her. It was never to be.

He checked into the hotel and went to the beach and sat on a chair. Few people were on the beach sunbathing and fewer in the water. It would be spring soon, but it was still chilly. He watched for and hoped he would see the fortune teller on the beach. He paid her no mind before, but he remembered seeing her almost every day when he was with Clare. Why would today be any different. No such luck, no fortune teller. Maybe she was further down the beach or at a different beach. But, tomorrow was a new day, maybe his lucky day. He would wait and he would eventually see her.

He had been swimming and walked to the shore. He had seen the woman for the last three days. She approached him and wanted to tell him his fortune. It would only cost him ten dollars. He saw an unkempt black woman with what he believed wild unruly hair, dressed in clothes he believed needed to be washed and breasts almost exposed. Peter thought her to be a bag lady. He brushed her aside and never spoke to her. He had no money on him. The following day he saw Clare with this strange woman and it appeared that they were having a disagreement about something. When he got closer he heard them argue about who had the better baseball team, Detroit, or Tampa Bay. He knew very little about either team. Peter may have played baseball in high school, but he didn't follow any major baseball team. He paid very little if any time on the newspaper sport page. He believed that Clare knew less than he did. But here she was, arguing with the bag lady. Clare would not relent, and the bag lady screamed at her, "Daphne DuBois puts a curse on you." He saw her kick sand at Clare and curse her. "May Maman Brigitte and all the gods of Haiti follow you and see that you are never happy." She then shook what was a bag of something at Clare, turned around and left in a huff.

"What was that all about?" he asked Clare.

"She wanted to tell me my fortune. I called her a hoax. Somehow we began arguing about baseball teams. That was when she told me she knows because she is a voodoo priestess. I laughed at her and told her if she was a priestess, she was most likely defrocked. She was no more a fortune teller or voodoo priestess than I was. She then cursed the Tampa Bay Rays, said they would never win a championship. She believed I was from Florida and knew something about the Rays, maybe a fan. All I knew of them is what I continually hear on the radio and them ready after spring training or read in the paper. I had no response when she said the best team was the Detroit Tigers. So, I, in turn, cursed them. She in turn nullified the curse I made. Said Detroit would win a championship. After that I believe you heard and saw the rest."

For the remainder of their stay in Florida, they saw the fortune teller, who Peter now openly referred to as the Bag Lady, but she always stayed clear of them on the beach. She never came near the area in which they were sunbathing or swimming. When their week was up, they left Florida. On their car trip to Florida they stayed on I-10 hoping to see the gulf. They rarely saw the water on their drive to Florida from the interstate. When they were to return home they decided to take a leisurely drive and meander through several southern states and enjoy the food and culture. They were introduced to different specialties of the south, but Clare usually wouldn't try them, not even southern fried chicken. Thought it would be greasy and too fattening. Boiled peanuts, disgusting! After several days they returned to Denver.

At the end of the third day, Peter still had not seen the bag lady, fortune teller. When he left Texas, he believed he had suppressed his thoughts about spells and curses, but here he was looking for a fortune teller. One who called herself a fortune teller, able to cast spells, put a curse on you. One he only met briefly and had no direct contact with. Maybe she had moved to a different location, further south, the beach in front of a different hotel. During the morning of his fourth day, as usual, a member of the staff, Ray, came to him and asked if he could get Peter something to drink. If he ever needed anything just ask for him. Peter usually asked Ray for a beer in the afternoon, but this morning he asked for a glass of fresh squeezed orange juice. When the drink was brought to him, he asked Ray about her, "Is she still around, the fortune teller? I believe she said her name was Daphne."

At first Ray didn't know who he was talking about. After a description and some prodding Ray said, "You must mean Anita. No. She's not around. She was arrested, caught stealing, going through people's clothes on the beach plus the hotel had complained to the police that she was harassing its patrons. I believe she was sent to jail for three years," Ray told him.

Peter was surprised but asked, "If I wanted to see her, how would I go about it? Is she in a local jail?"

"I'm not sure why you would want to meet her," said Ray, "but if you do, I would start with the local police department. They were the ones who arrested her. See what they say. They could most likely steer you in the right direction."

His GPS found the local police station and he drove to it. At the police station Peter talked to the desk sergeant. He said, "I knew the fortune teller, Daphne DuBois from Haiti, and would like to visit her. I've been told that she has been arrested. Where exactly is she incarcerated?" He said nothing of the curse.

"You are not her lawyer, are you?"

"No," Peter replied. "But if I wanted to talk to her, how would I go about it."

"Just how well do you know her?" the desk sergeant asked Peter.

"I didn't know her well but told her I'd look in on her next time I was in Naples," he replied.

"She may have gone by that name, Daphne DuBois, but it was an alias," the sergeant said. "Her real name is Anita Coos and before you say anything else, she is not from Haiti, but Detroit. She is in the Collier County jail. I believe that soon she will have served her minimum sentence and I believe then she will be extradited back to Detroit on a burglary and drug charge. Check with the jail, they will be able to give you visiting hours."

Peter was shocked by what he heard but tried hard not to show it. "So, her whole fortune telling ploy was a scam?"

The sergeant eyed him with a laugh behind the smile. "Did she fool you? If she did, you were not the only one. We estimated that she took in close to a hundred dollars on a good day. She couldn't foretell the weather after she heard the weather report, let alone people's fortunes. She was an interesting character, and she may have made for some interesting stories when hotel patrons returned home, but telling fortunes was not one of them."

The look on his face told the desk sergeant Peter was disappointed, neither had anything else to say. He thanked the sergeant and left the police station. In his car he found the Naples library. He punched it's address into his GPS and drove to it. He had decided to do some follow up research on Anita Coos, aka Daphne DuBois. As soon as he typed her name into the library's computer her name came up. He opened the first article which was in the local newspaper. It basically said what the police sergeant had told him, Anita Coos, who locally was known as Daphne DuBois a local beach fortune teller, was arrested for stealing from people's clothes on the beach. At her trial she was sentenced to three years but would get out in less than two years. Then she would be sent back to Detroit where she was wanted on burglary and drug charges. In Detroit it was believed that she ran a meth operation and was possibly implicated in the death to two teen age boys who died from drug overdoses. He opened the second article. It revealed that Anita Coos had been first arrested when she was eighteen on a drug and prostitution charge. She was the fourth of six children and lived in a single parent home. As he read he found that she had been in and out of jail for the last fifteen years. More investigating told him she skipped out on bail and was wanted. He read nothing that indicated that she had ever been to Haiti nor had relatives who lived there. Peter concluded that he had been completely taken in by a con artist and Clare's statement that her curse on Daphne was just as valid as Daphne's was on Clare. He believed she could not, would not be the witch in his life, lift the curse off him, if it was a curse. How gullible had he been. When he made that decision he realized that he was naïve, had begun to believe of a witch in his life. Peter was not acting like an adult, an educated man. He would return to Denver and to reality. There were root doctors, as Mary Ellen had said, but there was no such thing as witches. When he made the decision he also decided not to begin an investigation into the backgrounds of the latest women in his life, something he thought about when he learned about the beach fortune teller. Then the thought crossed his mind, what if what Mary Ellen had told him was true, he would ask the women in his life directly, and they would answer him truthfully. His idea about forgetting about a witch in his life began to waffle. It became his dominant concentration. Then he decided he would forget about such nonsense. There would be no witch in his life and somehow he would come to grips with his dream situation and learn to deal with it.

Peter decided that his trip, first to the sleep/dream research clinic and then to Florida was a big waste of time and money. He called Justine and told her he would be back to work on Monday. When she asked for details of his trip he told her he would tell all when he returned. He looked forward to being back home. He packed his few items of clothes and wondered if he should keep the pajamas that he bought when he planned to go to the sleep clinic. Yes. Why not. He took a quick look at a map of Florida. He would drive straight north on I-75 and swing west when it crossed I-10. He would follow it all the way to and through Texas to New Mexico. He would reverse the trip he took when he drove to Florida. He had no interest in seeing more of any of the southern states. The sooner he got home, the better he thought as he lingered over the hotel's breakfast. It was mid-morning before he was back on the road.

Chapter 10

His trip home was uneventful for the first day. There didn't seem to be much traffic on the interstates and he had made good time. He didn't see much of Alabama nor Mississippi. He passed through these two states quickly and only stopped in Mississippi for gas, and a quick something to eat at a McDonalds attached to a gas station. He stayed at a motel overnight just over the Louisiana border. No dream or plea. Maybe the sleep/dream clinic had done him some good. When Peter thought about it, no dreams since he left the clinic. The next morning he was up and on his way. He had not asked his GPS for instructions on how best to get to Denver and had turned it off. Peter didn't need instructions he would continue on I-10 until he would reach I-25 and then through New Mexico and to Denver. There was a lot more traffic when he reached Baton Rouge, but he was able to pass through the city with no trouble. He was hoping to reach Texas before he would stop and spend the night, but not in San Antonio. Then he heard it. His GPS told him to take the next exit. He thought that he had turned it off. Without giving it much thought, he believed the GPS was giving him good advice. Maybe there was road construction ahead or a bad accident that he should avoid. He ejected the disc he had been listening to so that he could hear further instructions. It never dawned on him how his GPS was able to be heard over the disc that he had been listening to. He passed over the interstate he had been traveling on and could see traffic going west. Why had he been instructed to exit? When he looked around on the new highway he was now traveling he wondered, why there weren't more cars? Surely he wasn't the only driver to be diverted. He made the decision that as soon as possible he would turn around and return to the interstate. After several miles he was instructed to turn again, then again and again. Somewhere he believed that he had made a mistake turning or the GPS was wrong. He had heard tales about drivers getting instructions to drive into a lake or onto a non-existent street. Once when he was driving west on I-10 into the Colorado mountains, at a road construction site, he was detoured. When he got back to I-10 which he had been detoured from, his GPS told him to turn east, which would have taken him back to Denver. But on this day, he blindly followed the GPS instructions until he believed that he was lost.

He saw a lot of water, swamp areas, and trees, no other vehicles, or houses. He didn't think he would remember all the turns he was instructed to make in order to return to the interstate, but he believed he would try to find his way back. He succeeded in becoming more lost. It was becoming late and he needed to find a place to stay. He came to an intersection, rather a Y in the road. He didn't remember it, so he continued going straight. After several minutes he saw a sign for the town Brigit de Ville, pop. 1,913. He drove into the town and saw a restaurant-bar-general store-gas station attached to a hotel. At least the sign above the door to the general store said hotel. A large sign above the gas station said Cooney's Corner. It looked familiar. Had he been here before? Peter wasn't sure, but the place was a haven. He parked and was ready to go inside when he caught sight of the hours for the store, gas station and hotel, 6:30 am - 11:00 pm. He went inside. The woman behind the counter wore a name tag, Grace, and she asked, "Can I 'elp youse?"

"Yes. I'd like a room for the night." He gave her his credit card when she asked for it. His room was on the second floor and there was no elevator. He would get his suitcase later. When he was checked in he asked about the restaurant and its food and where the restroom was.

"Down the 'allway, you can't miss da men's room. Just beyond it trew da door to the restaurant. If youse are ungry, it will aft to do. There is nutten else in town. Don't take what I said da wrong way, I tink it's good and eat dere a lot." He was handed two keys.

He was about to follow her instruction when he asked, "What does a person do after eleven o'clock if you close down?"

"Dey wait till morning or move on. You go out after eleven, can't get back in. Place locked up. One of da keys will fit door in back. Let youse into da hotel. Door to and from da store locked."

Peter thanked her and moved toward the restroom. When he came out he headed to the restaurant. When he opened the door, he was met with a cloud of cigarette smoke. The people obviously had not heard about the dangers of smoking or the ban in all public buildings. He sat at a table and looked around. He saw maybe eight people at the bar, two, he would venture to say, were not of legal drinking age and he saw two couples at other tables. A waitress brought him a glass of water, a one-page menu and told him she was Beverly and would be his waitress. "Da specialty of da house today is jambalaya served with catfish and cole slaw." She left and said she would be back in a moment. Then he saw it. A chalk board sign above the doorway to what he believed was the kitchen behind the bar area. Written on it was the restaurant's alligator menu breaded, deep fried, broiled, beer battered, Cooney's special, or a sandwich. He had seen it before when he was with Clare. He had not remembered Cooney's Corner or the restaurant until he saw the chalk board and its alligator special meals.

He wanted to try an alligator sandwich, but Clare absolutely refused to eat in the restaurant and insisted they leave. Not waiting for him, she turned and started for the door. He followed.

On their way to their car they saw an old, white haired woman coming out of the general store. As soon as she was outside, three young boys, the oldest maybe ten, began to taunt her. They had been making fun of her and attempted to take her cloth bag of groceries. He saw her swing at them with the cane that she had been using. He saw her hit one of the boys with her cane. It made him mad and all three boys were more determined than ever to grab her groceries. He was about to say something when Clare grabbed him by the arm and began to pull him toward their car. He saw the kid who was hit with the cane now grab it and pull it away from the woman. She fell, her grocery bag hit the ground and most of its contents spilled out and her glasses came off. All three of the boys now stood above her and he saw one spit at her. The boy who had taken the cane was now about to hit her with it. Peter pulled away from Clare, yelled and went toward the fallen woman. Clare shouted to Peter to come back but he continued toward the woman. The three boys, when they heard a man yell at them to leave the old woman alone, and saw him coming toward them, all three ran away. The one who had taken her cane dropped it. He could hear Clare calling to him, "Leave her alone, she will be all right."

Peter continued until he reached her, bent over, and asked, "Are you okay?" She mumbled what he thought was that she was okay and put out his hand to help her up. He felt long boney fingers grasp his hand. When she was standing he saw an elderly woman in a buttoned up to her neck dress with long sleeves, snow white hair fell to almost her waist. What he could see of her feet was vintage laced up shoes. Peter picked up her cane and handed it to her. Next, he gathered up her groceries, put them back in her cloth bag with hand strap handles and handed it to her. He saw her glasses, bent, and picked them up and held them out to her. She was standing, leaning on her cane, and had trouble putting her glasses back on since she held her cane in one hand and the bag with her groceries in the other and couldn't reach the glasses side pieces to her ears and put them on, unless she let go of her cane. Peter helped her by pulling one of the temple side pieces around her ear, she managed the other. He thought she looked unsteady, so he held her elbow.

Peter looked for Clare and saw that she had gone to their car. He had intended to ask her to help him with the old woman. Too late. What to do? Should he leave her as Clare had suggested? No. He took her grocery bag from her, took her by her free arm and started toward his car. As he walked with her, he told her, "I'll drive you home." She said nothing but allowed him to guide her and help her. When they reached his car, he opened the rear door and helped her to get in. He reached into the console and took a bottle of water from it. The bottle of water was warm, but he offered it to her when she stuck her hand out. She took the bottle and drank. She wiped her mouth and handed the bottle back. When she was settled on the back seat he saw her put out her arms for her bag of groceries which he was glad to give her. He got in the driver's seat, started his car and was about to ask which way. But first he told her to buckle up. He saw a puzzled look on her face and realized she didn't know what he was talking about. Peter ignored what he said about the seat belt, reached back and buckled her in. Satisfied he asked, "Which way?"

All he heard was, "Go." He began to move in the direction the car was pointed. He had gone maybe a half mile and was out of the town when he heard, "Here." He was not quite sure if this was where she wanted out because there was nothing around, not a house in sight. On both sides of the road he could see swamp and trees. He slowed down, turned around and looked at her. She repeated, "Stop! Here!" When he glanced at Clare he saw a disdained look on her face.

He pulled to the side of the road and stopped. "Is this where you want me to stop?" Her bag of groceries on the floor between her legs he saw her struggle with the seat belt release with one hand and the door handle as she tried to open the door. He turned the car off, unlocked the doors, got out and opened the door for her, then the seat belt release, picked up her bag of groceries and helped her out. Peter believed she had never ridden in a car that used seat belts. When she was out of the car she thanked him and referred to him as a young man. Still not sure what she was going to do, he waited. She seemed to gather herself and started back on the road. She walked close to fifty feet, turned, crossed the road and walked into the trees. He asked her again if she was okay, all she did was give a half turn and smiled at him. He told her he would help her if she needed him. She did not acknowledge his request. He watched her go with a steady, purposeful gait until she was hidden by the trees.

Back in the car he turned around and headed back toward the town. Clare was silent. He told her he had no idea where the next place would be where they could stop and eat, she didn't care. Told him to keep driving and about an hour later they came to another small town with a restaurant. They stopped, went inside, and ordered. While they waited, Clare wanted to know, "Why were you so concerned about an old woman you did not know and would never see again? It was none of your business, our business, what was happening."

He thought about it for a second and simply answered, "It was the Christian thing to do." Clare reminded him that he was not religious, he had told her he hadn't been in a church since he was eleven. He didn't know what the Christian thing to do was. The subject concerning the old woman never came up again and he believed they both had forgotten it.

The waitress Beverly came to his table and asked if he was ready to order. He decided on an alligator dinner. "I'm willing to try the strange meat. Too many items on your menu I don't know what they are. Dirty rice or rice and gravy both sound disgusting." He ordered fries with the grilled alligator and waited. His dinner arrived but he was hesitant to try it but believed if it were bad they wouldn't serve it. He took a forkful and put it into his mouth and began to chew. He thought the alligator was not bad. A little chewy but it was like over cooked chicken.

When he finished eating Beverly came to his table and asked, "What da ya think of gator?"

"I believe it tasted like chicken," he replied.

"What don't?" she said to him. She gathered up his dirty dishes and asked, "Will you 'ave desert? We 'ave some good pie."

"No. Just bring me my check." Peter watched her leave and she soon returned with his bill.

He paid with his credit card and she went to the register. He left her a big tip. When she picked up his receipt she saw the amount of the tip. "Thank youse very much and enjoy your stay here." He hesitated to get up from his table and Beverly noticed his hesitation. "Is dere someting else youse need?" she asked him.

"I was here almost a year ago, didn't eat in the restaurant but ran into an old woman with long white hair who had been grocery shopping. She carried her groceries in a greenish canvas bag. She used a cane. Do you know her, know who I'm talking about?" Why did he ask the waitress about the woman? It happened almost a year ago, what did he care who she was.

Beverly gave him a big smile and said, "You mus ta be 'ferring to Sofianna."

"Never caught her name," he replied.

"She live 'bout half mile or more outsid'a of town?" Beverly replied.

"Yes. She had me drop her off outside of town. She lives somewhere out there in the swamp?" he asked.

"Yep. Just follow da path and 'll take you right to 'er place," she said. "I've never been 'er place. Heard it's no more 'an a shack 'bout ready to fall down. Way 'fore my time built by two Brecht brothers. Dey hunt, fish, trap. Den, one up an die, udder move away. Anna move in bout year later. Said reltive and live dere since. Say she own it. No one ever question 'er."

"How does she manage to live?" he asked.

"Mighten get some money from da govment, don't know. I know she get money from people 'round here, and some work, specially from some of da Cajuns, some blacks. Either here in town or dey come over da swamp to see 'er. 'Ear dey come fer away as Nor'leans. Even from Missippi and 'Bama. They pay 'er. Some do chores for 'er or she hire men here. Why youse so interested in 'er?" Beverly wanted to know.

"I'm not, but since I kind'a met her, thought I'd ask." As an afterthought he asked, "Why would people pay her? Pay her for what?"

"Cause most people 'round here refer to 'er as Anna da Witch. Pay fo' spells an such. Frien' Marsalla swear by 'er. Got a herb, put in Mitch's drink. Less than two-month dey marry up. Doon need better or more proof," the waitress said, smiled and left Peter at his table.

Chapter 11

Peter walked back through the door that led him to the store and hotel. He went to his car and got his one suitcase. He smelled her, Jannette. Was it possible that she was here? No. It must be some bush or flower and the thought of her was soon dismissed. When he returned to the store, and he assumed the hotel lobby, Grace, the woman who checked him in, was still behind the store counter. She started up a conversation with him, where was he from, what kind of work did he do, why was he in Louisiana, will he be in town long. He answered all her questions easily. Then it was his turn, the talk with his waitress about a witch had renewed his interest in one. He put out of his mind the promise he had made to himself to forget about what Mary Ellen had told him and to return to Denver and live in the twenty first century. "What is that sweet smell I noticed when I came in?"

"Dat nite jasmine. Neva seen it blossom dis early fore. Lot of it aroun, less, deeper inta da swamp," she answered.

"Smells like lilac to me."

"Don know what lilac smell like," Grace replied.

When he finished talking about the sweet smell he asked about what he wanted to know, "Tell me about Anna the Witch."

"What's dere to tell?" Grace said and was silent for a moment. She stared at Peter and asked, "Who toll you 'bout 'er?"

"Beverly in the restaurant. Why is she called a witch?" he asked.

"Cause she casts spells, charms, incantations, makes potions, reads fortunes and all dat," Grace replied, "if you believe in all dat stuff. She 'posed to be a powerful witch. Can cas' spell on you quicker den a gator can snap his mouth shut."

"I do. Where can I get more information about her? Is there someone I can talk to?" he asked Grace.

"Talk to Cooney, owner, opens up da place early mornin'."

When he got to his room he believed that it had been a room in a large house which was now referred to as a hotel. He believed the store which also served the gas station was added to the house. In Colorado it would have been referred to as a bed and breakfast. One minor inconvenience, he had to use the bathroom down the hall. He was satisfied that it was a room and the bed was comfortable.

That night he opened the window and he could get a whiff of the night jasmine and again he thought about his neighbor in Denver. This night no bad dreams but one he had never had before. He was walking on the sidewalk back home in Denver. On both sides of it was water and in front of him was a blonde wearing a bikini top and cut off shorts. He tried but could not catch up to her. The faster he moved she was always ahead of him. Then he was fishing, and she appeared on the other side of the water. It was not a stream that he remembered ever having fished in. Then he saw her, and she looked at him and he saw it was not his neighbor Jannette. She was just a woman he didn't know. Not his dream woman. That was all that he remembered about the dream but the next morning he felt his unknown woman was thankful that he came. Why did he feel that? He had not dreamed about his unknown woman, but who, his neighbor Jannette? No. He did not know who the woman was or why he dreamed about her. The more he thought about the feeling he had that his unknown woman was thankful, the stronger it seemed to become. Why? He soon forgot about Jannette. What now, he asked himself. Back to his plan. Get up early and get on his way home.

It was beginning to get light outside. It had rained during the night, but he never heard it. He went to close the window and there wasn't a smell of jasmine. But he remembered it and the thought of his neighbor returned. Maybe he should ask her out when he returned to Denver. No, he thought. What would his analyst say? Peter soon dismissed both.

He went downstairs with his suitcase and decided to have breakfast in the restaurant if he was going to try and drive all the way to Colorado. On his way to the restaurant he saw a man behind the hotel/store counter. He was middle age, lanky, clean shaven, wore coveralls and a baseball cap. As soon as Peter approached him the man spoke, "You da guy Grace toll me 'bout?"

"If you are Cooney, yes," Peter answered.

Cooney picked up a sign from the counter, 'In the Restaurant' with an arrow pointed toward the restaurant. "Let's go. You can buy me coffee." When they entered the restaurant, Peter saw half a dozen patrons at the bar, some drinking what he believed was coffee and several eating breakfast. The woman behind the bar had given Cooney and Peter both a cup of coffee without being asked. Cooney led Peter to a booth that faced a monitor that displayed the store/lobby. "Anyone come in, I see."

"I see a few people eating at the bar. Surprised they are up so early," Peter said.

"Yeah. Eid'er fishermen, crawers, or loggers. See more when gator season." Cooney said.

Peter asked, "What's a crawer?"

"Men and women who dip for mud bugs, catch crawfish," Coney answered. He paused as he blew across his coffee and then took a sip, then asked, "What you want know 'bout Anna?"

Peter was hesitant about wanting to know more or anything about someone who didn't exist. He had time to think about her being a witch and decided to believe she was just a woman who lived alone in the swamp so, people around made-up tales about her. She might be an old woman with long white hair, the one thing she wasn't, was a witch. He had returned to the decision he made before he left Florida. There was no such thing as a witch and there were none in his life. He would not investigate the backgrounds of women in his life. Instead of forgetting about Anna, he looked at Cooney across his cup of coffee and simply replied, "Tell me about her."

Cooney began. "Not much ta tell. Live in da swamp. Been 'round for ev'a. Say she 'lated to the Brecht brothers. Now her place. No body eve question er."

"Why is she called a witch?" Peter asked.

"'Cause she one. Casts spells some fortunes, dat why," was Cooney's reply, "not like dem voodoo priests back near Nor'leans an all der mumbo-jumbo."

Peter thought that he had heard enough. If it wasn't a hoodoo from the mountains, a fortune teller on the beach it was now an old woman who lives in the swamp and casts spells. He didn't say or ask anything else, finished his coffee and thanked Cooney for his time and got up to leave and laid three-dollar bills on the table. He was not going to have breakfast. The sooner he was on the road, the better. Before he could reach for his suitcase and go he heard Cooney say almost as an afterthought, "And she dance wit da devil."

"What? Why did you say that?" he asked.

Cooney looked at him with a smile on his face and seriously said, "It true."

"You've seen her do that?" Peter asked.

"Nah. But hear it from otters. She dance wit devil," Cooney replied.

"What do you mean she dances with the devil?" Peter asked. He had heard and read about this aspect of witches before. His search on the internet concerning witches showed mainly women dancing around a fire or in the moon light. Several with an unidentifiable being or a man with horns, who Peter believed was meant to represent the devil. His interest in Anna the Witch was changed. He sat back down. "Tell me about it, her," he said to Cooney.

"What to tell. Dark of da moon she dance wit da devil," Cooney replied.

"Not in the moon light?" Cooney remained silent. "If you've not seen her do this, how do you know?" Peter asked.

"People talk. How know. Eveyone round here know Sofianna do it," was his short reply.

The restaurant waitress came to their table with a coffee pot and refilled their cups. When she left Peter said, "Explain it to me. What is dark of the moon?"

"Night no moon. Night between old moon and new moon. Once a month. Thursday night, tonight be dark of moon. Devil an demons bout. Everyone stay inside. Otters try to see what she do, never hear from or see 'gain. Maybe drown in swamp, gator et em. No one try to see again, long time," Cooney said as he sipped his coffee.

This was an aspect of a witch Peter had never heard. He thought they met during the full moon, at least they did in the movies. That was some writer or director's idea. But the dark of the moon, every month was what Cooney said and got him interested in witches again. Ms. Schwarz believed his dreams were more intense once a month. Not about getting a woman pregnant but his dreams had to do with the cycle of the moon. "Tell me about her spells, her curses. Are they for real? What makes you believe that she does them? That they happen?" Peter wanted to know.

Cooney just smiled at Peter and shook his head up and down. "Dey true. 'Bout year go, tree boys tease her, try steal groceries. Less month one breaks arm, other breaks leg, always limp."

"And what about the third boy?" he wanted to know.

"He get fever, in a com'," was the answer Peter got. He continued, "Year later still no well, no awake."

"Think she can stop bad dreams?" Peter wanted to know. He heard the sincerity in Cooney's voice, why not humor Cooney.

"Have ask her. Maybe. She tell ya," Cooney replied.

Peter was caught up in what this man had been telling him. He asked, "How do I go about seeing her? She come into town often?"

"No. Youse stay way, you ask for trouble. You no wanna see. Almost dark of moon, to nite. No time be out, near her. Devil be 'bout nite. Everyone stay in, lights out, doors locked. Better youse go back where came from. Stay away from Anna da Witch," Cooney replied.

The advice came too late. Peter had made up his mind to find and see this witch and find out if she could help him with his dreams. He had gone to a reincarnation group, a medium, a root doctor, spent a lot of money on an analyst, a dream research clinic, and an urge to drive to Florida to look for a fortune teller, why not see a supposed witch. Someone everyone knew was a witch. See what it would cost, a spell to stop his dreaming, his nightmares. Couldn't be very much. If his dreams were just that, dreams and not real, something from his past, could she help or if he believed that she helped, would the dreams stop? Why not find out. If she could convince him she was real, then a placebo spell could work.

"Cooney, how do I find her place in the swamp?" Cooney didn't answer but got up from the table and started back toward the store. Peter followed him. When he was behind the counter Peter begged him to help find Sofianna. "Please, I need to have a spell, a curse lifted."

"No, not know what happen me I do. You stay away!"

Peter decided to stay another day. He had breakfast, had put his suitcase in his car but would get it later and walked around the town for a while. It was chilly but not cold enough to require a jacket. When the sun got above the horizon it was warm. Like what the temperature had been in Florida. He returned to the restaurant near noon. Beverly was working. When she went to the table where Peter was sitting he asked, "Beverly, how do I find the path to Sofianna's?"

"Misser, you don't go there," she replied. "Tonight, dark of moon. Be dangerous. The devil be 'bout."

"Tell me. I do want to see her!" he said with some urgency in his voice.

Beverly hesitated but finally said, "Quarter mile or so outta town, soon cross bridge, see big, big tree. Jus' pass it, utter side of road, see path. Follow, don't get off or lost. Dat real bayou country out ta der. Groun wet ad slippy. Maybe cotton mouths in da water. You fall, maybe bit by one or gator et youse if'n youse fall in'a swamp. Never find."

Peter thanked her and headed for his car. He remembered the direction he had taken when he drove the old lady and drove out of the town. He soon crossed the bridge, that he didn't remember, and there it was, a huge tree. It could have been a cottonwood, he wasn't sure. He drove to the side and well off the road and parked. Got out of his car and crossed the road. The first thing he became aware of was the smell. It wasn't like a rain in Denver, a fresh smell that made him aware of the soil. This was a stale, decaying smell. It was a combination of decaying plant life and the stagnant water of the swamp. An occasional quick and slight breeze of wind would clear the air, blow the stench away but, on the other hand could blow more smell to him. He would deal with the smell. He would get used to it. In a short time, he became accustomed to the smell and didn't notice it.

He walked along side of the road all the while he looked for what would be a path. He soon found it and started to walk. He saw swampy areas on both sides covered with green what? Scum or he was sure some sort of plant life. He didn't know for sure nor care. As he walked the swamp on one side lessened and was replaced by ground and the smell was weaker. Now there were more trees and Peter heard a lot of strange noises he believed were made by birds. Peter saw a lot of them flying in the trees or saw them lift off from a patch of swamp that he could see, birds he had never seen before. Many insects flew around him, and mosquitos tried to bite him. Wasn't it too cold for them? Wasn't it still winter? But maybe warm enough in Louisiana. He heard something in the water splashing around, when he looked between the trees he didn't see anything, but a large area of the green was missing and the water in that area was covered with ripples. Two eyes above the water looked at him for a moment and then disappeared below the water. When he looked behind him he was unable to see his car and because of the rain last night, his feet felt wet. The sun was shining and would hopefully dry the ground, but now, his shoes and feet were wet and as Beverly said the ground was slippery. Easy to lose his balance and slip into the swamp. He believed that the path was going deeper into the swamp. The trees were becoming more plentiful. Ahead he saw something skitter across the path, but he couldn't identify it. To his right through the trees, he could see water. The path angled toward it and when he got nearer he saw that the swamp had given way to a large expanse of open water. Beverly told him many of Sofianna's visitors went to her over the swamp. To Peter it meant they went to her by boat, they couldn't get there any other way. He had walked what he believed was half a mile or more and on the embankment of the water and he could see a structure through the trees. He continued toward it. It was at an angle to the path and was on a small inlet of the lake. It was more than a shack; it was a cabin on what could be considered high ground. If he had to describe it, he would say it was built by a movie construction crew and it was not ready to fall. There was a stack of cut firewood almost three feet high along the front wall to the side of the cabin beyond the cabin's small porch. There were no trees around the cabin, it was in a clearing. He remembered how old and frail she had looked, too old to have cut the wood. If what Beverly had said about people helping her, someone else had cut her wood. Open water was at its front with a small dock. The open water had gotten shallower and gave rise to plant life and the green scum that he had seen on his walk to the cabin, swamp at what would be the far side of the cabin, maybe a hundred feet away. Before one would reach the swamp there was a small structure, he assumed was an outhouse and most likely on the rear of the cabin would be a door. A fast way to the outhouse, not a long walk from the front and around the cabin. There were no tree stumps, meant that trees had been removed or were not allowed to grow. He became aware that he no longer could smell the swamp. Was it a slight breeze that blew the smell away or had he become so used to it that he didn't notice it?

He went to the cabin from the lake side, the front. There was a small roof over a small porch being held up by square rough-cut porch posts. On one of the posts was a hurricane lantern. The building's door was open. He looked into a black hole. He stopped; he wasn't sure if he should go to it, but he began to walk. He reached the porch of the building and stopped. He called out, "Sofianna, I'm here to see you, need your help, a spell." He waited and there was no answer. She didn't hear him. Maybe she wasn't home. He stepped onto the porch, walked around the hurricane lantern, and called out again. He waited. He was about ready to knock at the side of the door when from the side of the house the old woman appeared.

"I was around side, tending to my garden," she said. "What I do for you?"

Peter looked at her and remembered the white hair. This time it was twisted in a bun on the rear of her head and when she turned around he could see a silver hair pin in the shape of butterfly wings stuck through it. Before he hadn't paid much attention to her but now he looked more closely. She was old, could pass for anywhere between sixty and a hundred. Her eyes were dark, almost black. What he could see of exposed flesh was well tanned, wrinkled and she was thin. Her clothes were old but clean and she wore an apron that was soiled. Her dress sleeves had been rolled to above the elbows, her hands were dirty and muddy from digging in the soil, her feet were bare. She had a warm smile when she talked to him and he could see good teeth. He believed that most likely they were false to look that good. He answered her, "I need a spell."

"Come into my house. First we talk about cost." She stepped onto the porch, went to a bucket with water on a small bench and washed her hands. She dried them in her apron. Before they entered the cabin she wiped her bare feet on a rug. Peter did the same and they walked through the open doorway. When his eyes became accustomed to the dark interior, he could see the interior was sparse, clean, and well kept. On the one window there were curtains that kept out light. Beneath it was a hand crank windup Victrola and a small stack of vinyl records, old seventy-eights. He could see several books on a shelf under it, too dark to make out any titles. There was a door on one wall that he assumed led to the bedroom. On the wall to either side were burnt candles in wall sconces. To the side of the door, was he assumed, a wood burning old cook stove and a counter. In a box near the stove were several pieces of firewood and kindling. In the counter was a sink that had an old fashion hand pump. Above the counter were shelves and he could see a small assortment of pots, pans of different sizes, dinnerware, and cups. From a rafter near the shelf were several bunches of what he thought were dried weeds. Scattered around the interior in addition to the wall sconces were a few candles. Near the center of the room was a table with two chairs. On the table were a kerosene oil lamp, a candle and he was able to recognize a bible. Should a witch have a bible? No. Well, maybe. No one ever said they were not religious. It was always assumed they were in league with the devil. The one who lived next door to him wore a necklace with a cross and Mary Ellen said some were religious. He needed to stop thinking of Jannette as a witch. She was just a woman, not a witch. And Anna, just an old woman. People may think of her as strange, lived alone in the swamp but she was not a witch. A third chair was propped against the open door, he assumed, to help keep it from swinging closed. There was no screen door. How would she keep the different types of insects Peter had seen out?

Sofianna sat and invited Peter to do the same. "You most likely don't remember me, but I met you about a year ago."

It may have been sunny outside, but it was dim in her cabin even though the open doorway allowed light form outside. Sofianna pulled open a drawer in the table, took out a match and lit the lamp on the table. She reached into the drawer and brought out a pair of wire framed glasses Peter remembered she wore. Before he could say anything else, she looked at him and held up her finger to her lips, indicating that he be quiet. She whispered, "Close the door."

When he got up, so did she. He went to the door and she went to the Victrola, wound it up and put a record on it. He could hear a recording artist. The record was scratchy and the artist, Peter believed had a twangy voice whom he had never heard before singing about a cheating heart. Peter removed the chair and pulled the door toward him. He saw it. Carved into the door was the symbol, an upside down cross in a circle with two horizontals, one inside the circle and the other outside it. He momentarily froze. He felt a hand touch his arm and a quiet whispered voice say, "Make sure the door is closed tight." He couldn't move. Peter was close to having a panic attack. He hadn't taken either of his two anti-depressants since he left the dream clinic in Texas. His first thought was that he was having one of his dreams. Then he felt Sofianna reach around him and close the door and latch it and the symbol could no longer be seen. "Come," she whispered and took him by the arm. She had to pull Peter from the spot where he stood. He just stared at the closed door. He moved as she pulled him and led him to the table and his chair.

Peter sat and didn't say a thing. After a moment his heart wasn't racing and he calmed down, he asked, "The symbol, carved into your door, what does it mean?"

Sofianna looked across the table, her finger to her lips and whispered, "Nothing. One of cousins who built this cabin carved it years ago. Before my time. One on back door too."

He accepted her answer but Peter was puzzled, why did she wish them to be quiet? He was calm enough to now quietly ask, "Why are we whispering? There's no one around who could possibly hear us."

She whispered back, "The swamp. The swamp can hear us. We be quiet and with music, can't hear."

He believed her to be strange and was going to ask for a spell, so he listened to her. He would talk quietly to her if that was what she wished. "I've been told you can cast spells. I need you to cast a spell for me. What will it cost?"

She squinted at him and said, "I remember you. Hoped I'd never see you again. Will be no cost. What do you want? Money? Success? Someone to be sick? Hurt?"

Peter didn't answer her. He wondered why she hoped to never see him again. Why would she ever believe that he would come back to see her? He said, "I want you to help me sleep, quit having a certain type of dream."

She studied him closely and he wondered what color her eyes really were. They looked black and the flickering lamp light seemed to dance in them. "Cannot do," she replied.

"You can't cast a spell?" he asked her.

"Can cast a spell but it will do no good. Can't stop you having bad dreams."

"And why is that? How do you know I have bad dreams, nightmares?" he asked.

Sofianna hesitated for a while before she answered. "I thought you a wonderful young man who helped me. Didn't think much of your girlfriend. Cast a spell. Called on a spirit to go to you and give you what you need, not what you want. Why girlfriend left you. Didn't need her."

How did she know about Clare Peter wondered? Could be a lucky guess.

"Thought spell was over when I wished someone could help me. Why you get dreams. Spirits calling to you, need to come help me. They pull you toward me. Can't stop them. What you dream is real. Spirits see to it. Can't stop the dreams. You can't help me. All same spell."

"What are you talking about, spirits?"

"They everywhere, either in a person or close by, all need is way to talk to them, tell them what I want. Unless spell completed, will last long time. You can't help me, I can't stop your dreams," she answered him.

"Why can't I help you?" he wanted to know.

"Not a spirit. Much worse and much stronger, evil. Made an agreement with very long time ago. Won't let go of me. Can't be bargained with, bribed, threatened. Has hold of me," she replied. "You do nothing."

What was she talking about? Did he believe her? Why couldn't he help her? He could at least try. "Let me try. Let me help you," he replied.

"No. You go now, be dark soon. Can do nothing. Never come back again," Sofianna got up, went to the door and was about to prop it open as before. She hesitated, turned, and walked to the Victrola and lifted the arm with the needle. Peter remained seated as he watched her. She returned to the table and took him by the arm and pulled until he was in a standing position and she ushered him to the door. He gave up resisting her, she pulled the door open and began to push him out. Peter walked out of the cabin onto the porch and he saw that it was beginning to get dark, maybe the sun had set. No, it was cloudy there was no way to tell. He turned toward her and was about to plead to allow him to help when she said, "Go! Don't stop. Dark soon!" She closed the door on him.

Peter knew that she was serious, and he believed what she said. He stared at the closed door. The symbol carved into it stood out in the approaching darkness. Did he follow the symbol to here? Where was here? He was to reach his woman calling him to a cabin in the middle of a swamp in Louisiana and hear an outrageous, no, hear an unbelievable tale of spirits and spells. Listening to Sofianna was as bad as listening to Mary Ellen. Was this one of his dreams? Would he awake, get dressed and go to work? No. Peter was sure he was not dreaming. He reached out and grabbed a porch post and was sure he could feel the rough texture of the wood. He stepped off the porch and headed down the path he had followed to the cabin. It had grown chilly and he wished that he had worn a jacket.

The sounds were louder, especially he was able to recognize frogs calling. It was still the end of winter. Shouldn't frogs still be in hibernation or whatever they do in the wintertime? Apparently not in Louisiana. It seemed the cries and cackling of birds had stopped but the insects were worse. He could occasionally hear something splash in the water. After he had walked a hundred yards or so, he stopped and turned. He could just get glimpses of the cabin through the trees. He was not sure because he was so far away from it or because it was becoming dark. He wondered, what if it were true, local people believed she danced with the devil? Maybe she did dance in the dark, around a fire. But she did not dance with the devil. He began to walk, stopped, and decided he wanted to find out. Fighting off the mosquitos he turned around and walked back toward the cabin. He stood behind a large tree and could see through the trees so that he had a good view of the cabin. He then made a dumb decision to sit. The ground was wet and he got wet. Too late to do anything about it. He knew it was cloudy and he hoped it wouldn't rain. He would wait until it got dark. He looked out over the lake and could see what he thought was low hanging fog begin to form over the water. It seemed to change shape and what popped into his mind was it was a will-of-the-wisp, but it didn't keep a shape long enough and from what he knew of them there wasn't a light or glow with it. Peter watched it for a moment, and it reminded him of a face, but it wasn't a face. He tried to forget about it, settled back against the tree as he shivered and closed his eyes. Is this such a good idea he thought? No. But then nothing to do but wait. After five minutes and a dozen or more bug bites, Peter knew it wasn't a great idea, a bad decision. How ridiculous, a witch dancing with the devil. Do either exist? Peter decided he would leave while he could still see the path. He had to hurry if he were to get to his car. He began to get up and found that he had difficulty. He would wait a few minutes and try again. Had he allowed his leg to fall asleep? He massaged it. He closed his eyes. He waited and even though he was uncomfortable, cold, and wet, wasn't aware that he had nodded off. The last thing he remembered was the sounds of different frogs.

Chapter 12

It had begun to rain; it was a light rain and seemed to stir up the smell of rotting plant life. When he awoke, he couldn't see a thing. It was dark. He became aware of the smell again. It wasn't the rain that caused him to awaken or the cold but a loud noise. What was it? He didn't know. Maybe it was a frog near him. Most likely a bird. An owl? Maybe, most likely since it was night and dark. What had he been dreaming? He couldn't remember but it made him feel good even though he was now wet. He felt stiff, stretched, tried to shake off the cold and felt better. He couldn't see anything. It truly was the dark of the moon. He didn't even see stars. He asked himself why he decided to stay and find if Sofianna danced with the devil. It was ridiculous. Just as ridiculous as him wanting a spell and her granting it. Her talk about spirits, an aspect of witches he had never heard or read about. It was too farfetched. Better to get back to reality. And now it was too dark. He decided to leave, stood, but he was unable to find his way back to his car, couldn't find or see the path. Could he slip and fall into the swamp, become as Beverly said, an alligator's supper, be et by an alligator? Yes. And he was uncomfortable, he was wet and getting wetter, the swamp smell was stronger, and the chill had returned. Best to stay where he was and wait until morning. No. Return to Sofianna's cabin and if she wouldn't let him in, stay on her porch. At least get out of the rain. But Peter was not sure exactly where the cabin was, which way to go but he believed he knew which direction to go even though he was unable to discern the path that he had followed to her cabin.

Again, he leaned back against the tree, sat, and closed his eyes. He would try to sleep. Peter tried to get comfortable. The ground may have been wet, and the tree's leaves prevented him from getting soaked from the rain, but he knew he would be wet by morning. At least the rain kept the bugs away. It was not a warm night, but chilly enough to cause him to shiver. He thought about Denver, home, and fishing when he heard it again. Was it a yell, a squeal? It definitely was not a frog or any bird that he ever heard. He stood and looked beyond the tree, where he believed the sound came from and that's when he saw it. Off among the trees, and to where he believed Sofianna's cabin to be, he saw a warm colored glow, just like what he was used to seeing in his dreams. The first thing he asked himself, was this a dream? No. He felt his behind was wet and then something bites him, he knew this was not a dream. There was no silent plea for help like in his dreams. He would go to the glow. He was able to avoid the trees that were in his way because the trees temporarily blocked his view of the glow. As he got closer the glow became brighter. It was a fire. He could clearly see the cabin; the fire was to the rear and to the opposite side of it and lit up the cabin's rear. It would warm him if the rain wouldn't put it out.

When he was near the clearing and the cabin, he stopped at a tree and used it to hide behind. He had a clear view of the cabin and the fire. As he watched the fire, it didn't die down from the rain. Why didn't it? The fire seemed to be getting larger. Had the rain stopped? No. He was getting wet. As soon as the idea passed through his mind, he became aware that there was nothing feeding the fire. It was above the ground and seemed to exist without burning anything. Then he saw it, a misshapen something, a misshapen what? He didn't know. Did it come out of the swamp? Was it an animal? He didn't recognize it as an animal or person. It was unclothed. It circled the fire, occasionally walking on all fours and other times it was on its hind legs. His first thought was that it was a monkey. Occasionally he believed he could see through it. It was not any animal he had ever seen nor was it humanoid. Was it real? It was about four feet tall, its nose, it didn't have a nose but two nostrils in its face. There was no mouth or ears. Where the ears should have been he could see holes, like the non-existent nose. Peter wasn't sure if it had eyes. All that he could see were two black holes where the eyes would be. It was hairless and as far as he could see, sexless. Its hands were long with long fingers and nails like an animal. Its hind legs had long toes. He was sure it was not a monkey; it had no tail. If what Sofianna had told him was true, this creature had to be a spirit, no, the devil. Her tale of spirits could be true and Cooney's story of her dancing with the devil wasn't as far-fetched as he believed. He was going to go to it, challenge it. Peter tried but was unable to move. It seemed like his dreams; he was stuck to the ground. He was going to yell at it, but no sound would come out of his mouth. All he could do was watch, watched as the devil danced. It gave out a squeal occasionally, the sound that had awakened him. But it didn't have a mouth! As he watched he realized there were two of them. Was it possible that there could be two devils? Where did the second one come from? He believed there was only one. Occasionally they held hands and swung each other around as they circled the fire. Their faces opened to form a mouth. From their mouths came long, snake like tongues that quickly intertwined and then they pulled apart. As he watched they became one. How was that possible? The fire grew larger. Then they were apart and there were three of them, then four. They were not devils. Were they spirits? Where were they coming from? They were just materializing. One of them gave out a loud squeal, the sound that had awakened him. The four, no six continued to dance around the fire. They were coordinated as though they were dancing to unheard music that only they could hear. They stopped and stared at the cabin. Sounds came from them, squeaking sounds. Then a loud squeal from one of them. Different and louder than before. From the cabin's rear came Sofianna. Dressed as she had been when he first saw her, she approached the dancers. Two of the beings took her by her hands and began to circle the fire with her. As the dancers with Sofianna circled the fire Peter saw the other creatures begin to remove her clothes. Her dress wasn't unbuttoned, it was just pulled away from her and tossed to the side. He was both mesmerized and horrified by what he was seeing but he couldn't stop watching. As they slowly undressed her, pulled away several pieces of undergarments, the creatures nearest began to stroke her arms. One reached up, pulled the hair pin out of her hair and undid it. He saw Sofianna's white hair become undone and cascade behind her. When she was undressed he was able to see that at her age she was well preserved, her almost flat chest had withered breasts and her wrinkled face told him of her age. Her pubic area was white. Why did he focus on it, think it would be sexy? He watched as one after another stroked her body, touched her, rubbed up against her as she was being pulled around the fire by the creatures, not six but eight, then how many, he could only guess. As she circled the flames the fire grew, and she began to change. Her hair began to darken, her breasts began to become fuller, her wrinkled face became smooth. Peter was not sure if it was happening or did the darkness and fire light play tricks on him. How long it took he didn't know but dancing around the fire was a very good looking, young, attractive well-built woman with long black hair. He couldn't see but was sure her black eyes were now green. He had been so caught up in seeing her change he hadn't noticed that the spirits continued to grow until they completely encircled the fire, about twenty-five feet in diameter, and he was no longer cold. Could he be being warmed from the fire even though it was a good distance from it? If on cue the dancing stopped. The creatures formed a double line that led off to the cabin's side, beyond the outhouse, toward the swamp, all except the two that held Sofianna's hands. Through the darkness he could see the low hanging fog, the what he believed was the will-of-the-wisp. If that was what it was, it had moved. It was no longer out over the water where he had first seen it, but now it was on the backside of the cabin. As Peter watched it move, it came toward the fire and then it stopped moving when it seemed to reach the shore the double line of creatures had approached it, they too stopped at the swamp's edge. He could see it change color. Nearer the fire he could see that it had taken on the color of the green scum he remembered seeing on the stagnant water. It had become the scum. It began to move on land and upward. No. Something was pushing the green scum, pushing it up as though the ground was rising. Peter believed it was becoming a human figure, or did he imagine it? It became larger than the creatures and was made up of dirt, moss, roots, and anything that made up the earth by Sofianna's cabin. It left a trail of scum as it moved and reminded Peter of the trail left behind by a snail. But this was no snail. And the smell of the swamp became stronger or did a gust of wind blow from the swamp toward him? He didn't know and tried to dismiss the smell. But he couldn't. The smell was so strong it almost made him want to throw up. It made his eyes water and it stung his nose and throat. He remembered the time when he was younger and stumbled upon a dead and rotting deer. The stench stayed with him, and what he smelled now was the pungent smell of stagnant water and rotting vegetation. It reminded him of the smell of rotting and decaying flesh.

It appeared that the double row of creatures bowed as it passed them, and the fire continued to grow. What he thought were tree roots became legs and arms. The green scum dripped off it and revealed a human form. The scum from the swamp ran down its head and face, off its chest and arms. When it neared the fire Peter could see that this one was now human in size and appearance with the same facial features as the other creatures, there were no facial features. All the remnants of the swamp scum and earth had fallen away or changed. It reminded him of the image he saw in his dream. It was the devil. It was the He/It of his dreams. It did not have the often devil depicted with horns, red piercing eyes, a tail, cloven hooved feet, bat like wings or any of the other attributes associated with the devil. The He/It wasn't frightening to look at once he accepted the lack of human facial features. On the hands of the long arms and its feet it did have pointed nails, like the nails of an animal. It was easy for Peter to see that he was a male. He had an appendage that all the pictures of the devil did not have, a large hanging penis with oversized testicles. The creatures resumed their former positions, and they began to dance as before. The large creature was trying to get past the smaller ones in order to get to Sofianna, but she continued to be pulled further and further away from the creature. But he kept getting closer to her and as he did, Peter could see that he was becoming excited, his penis began to become firm. When he came almost to Sofianna. His erection stood straight out. The two creatures who held Sofianna's hands pulled her to the ground and he mounted her. As he moved in and out, the cadre of creatures cheered him on with loud squeaks and squeals. After a moment, the devil gave out a terrible scream and Peter believed it was when he climaxed. The devil got off Sofianna and as he did the fire began to die down and the small creatures began to disappear, but not this creature, the devil. He kneeled before her, between her spread legs and looked at her for a moment. Was He/It admiring her beauty? Gloating? Letting her know that she was his, would always be? He stood and turned. Peter thought that the devil looked directly at him and though the devil's face was expressionless, Peter believed he felt it smile at him. No. It was a sneer. In a moment the devil turned back and began to walk toward the swamp from where it came and was gone. It didn't just disappear. It seemed to meld into the earth, became the earth and swamp. First the legs appeared to turn, turn into earth and as the devil moved further, deeper into the swamp it became its surroundings, the earth and swamp. It was hip deep, then chest deep in the swamp until it was no more, and the-will-of-the-wisp formed above where the devil had disappeared. He would always associate the rotting vegetation smell with the devil, evil. No. Why did he think of what he had witnessed as evil? It may have been reprehensible, but was it evil? Peter didn't know, and then the smell was gone. Peter began to feel the chill of the night.

The fire was low and had almost disappeared. Peter thought that maybe he should go to her while he could still see Sofianna, but he couldn't bring himself to move. What would the spirits do, the devil do? Could they hurt him, kill him? The more he wanted to go to her the more difficult it became for him to move. Like in his dreams, he was unable to reach her. Unlike his dreams there was no plea for help. He could see Sofianna lying on the ground. Her hair was becoming white and it was becoming more difficult to see her in the dying fire, the enveloping darkness. The night was again becoming dark and quiet. Peter sat at the tree and was dumbfounded. There was no doubt in his mind that she truly danced with the devil. It stood to reason that the other things people said about her and what she did were also true. She was a witch, a sorceress. What could he do? Nothing. He was fixed to the ground and couldn't move, and he would be unable to change who and what she was. Then the fire was gone, and he was engulfed in the total darkness of the night.

At some point, even though wet, shivering, and uncomfortable, he had fallen asleep. A bird nearby was chirping, and it awakened him. His first thought was, did what he remember, what he saw, really happen? Or was he waking from another dream, a nightmare? When he looked to where the fire was, he saw nothing. No evidence that a fire had ever been there, nothing appeared burned and there were no ashes. Sofianna and her clothes were gone. Could an old woman be made to change into a young woman in a matter of a few minutes? No. In the movies, yes. But what he witnessed was not a movie. Did he imagine it? Yes. Did it happen? No. Would he be unable to move in real life? No. Maybe in a dream, but he was not awakening from a dream. But then he wondered, could it have happened? Maybe. If it did happen, would she still be young? He remembered that he saw her begin to age, age as the fire burned out. Or did he imagine it? He was not sure.

This morning he was able to move. He was going to find out. Peter was able to get up and he walked unsteadily to the cabin. The door was closed, and he could clearly see the symbol that for the past several months haunted him. Peter knocked on it. She opened the door and he saw an old woman standing in the semi darkness, dressed as before, she invited him in. She harshly whispered, "I told you to leave. You shouldn't have been a witness to what happened last night."

"What happened last night? I saw it but what did I see? Tell me! Explain it!" Peter pushed his way past her and stared at Sofianna. He waited for an answer, but one was not forthcoming. He continued to stare at her. He remembered what Mary Ellen had told him that a witch would have to answer if directly asked. "You must tell me. What did I see? Why? I'm not leaving until you do!"

Sofianna could see the determined look on his face and knew that he was serious. She closed and latched the door. It became dark in the cabin. She pulled him to the table, lit a candle on it and they sat. She whispered, "The swamp can't hear. Understand? As it says in the bible, the earth is his, he is the earth, deserts, mountains, swamp and water."

"Who is he? Who is the earth?" Peter wanted to know.

"Satan," was all that she said.

"It doesn't say that in the bible. Why are you saying it?" Peter whispered.

She had to shush him. She put her finger to her lips, they must be quiet. "From the beginning it was so. When Jesus was in the wilderness, Satan promised him he could rule all that he beheld. All that he would need to do was bow to Satan, worship him. How could he do that if the earth weren't his?"

Peter thought for a second and whispered back, "I don't understand, don't know the bible that well."

"Don't ask how or why," she said, "but every dark of the moon he comes to me. He turns me into a young woman, as I was years and years ago, and fills me with his seed, evil seed. He wants me to give him a son. A son who will grow into an evil man. Makes me believe that if I do what he wants, I will stay young and beautiful. But I won't. After he leaves, I eat a root from my garden that will kill a son if it should start to grow within me. He doesn't know. I will not give in to his wishes. I will not stay young."

"What if you don't come out when called?" he asked her.

"If I don't, he will send his minions, his demons, in for me and they will hurt me," she replied. "They rake me with their claws. The claw marks become infected and hurt. Become unbearable for weeks. They beat me. Broke my leg once. Now I heed their call."

"There must be something that can be done." With conviction in his voice Peter said, "I'll help you, move you away."

"No. He will find me. Moved from home, Lake De Cade area, up north hundred miles or more, he came. Moved here, he came. Impossible to get away from him. He is the earth, everywhere, so he knows, knows where I am when my feet touch the ground."

Peter was silent as he listened to her. What he heard about her was true so what she says is true. Maybe he should just leave. He hadn't solved his dream problem and according to her, would not. He began to shake his head no and whispered, "No," to what he was thinking and what he heard Sofianna say.

"I'm sorry for what I've done to you. You should leave, take good care of her. She is what you need. I hope to never see you again." Sofianna was silent, got up from the table and went to the door and opened it, propped the chair against it. She was finished talking to Peter and the open door was his invitation to leave. She returned to the table and blew out the candle.

He hesitated but finally got up and walked to her. She looked away when he tried to look at her. Peter walked through the doorway and started back toward his car. He will take her advice. She knew that he couldn't help her, and he had to accept that fact, just as she had to accept the devil, dance with him.

He had a lot to think about on his walk to his car and his drive back to the hotel at Cooney's Corner. Would his analyst believe him if he told her about Sofianna? No. He wouldn't tell her. She would believe he had become delusional. His dreams would not stop and what did she mean about sending him someone he needed, not wanted. Why Clare and he parted. Her final statement about taking good care of her. Had Sofianna sent Donna? He believed it must be so, just as Mary Ellen had said, and he let her go.

Back at the hotel Cooney was working. "You were not here last night. You go see her? See her dance wit da devil?"

Peter believed he would be quiet about what he had seen and heard. "Too unbelievable to be believable." As an afterthought he asked, "What can you tell me about the Lake De Cade area? Is it far from here?"

"Dat real bayou country. Youse wanna stay way from dere. Lotta snakes, gators and strange people." Cooney replied.

Chapter 13

Peter checked out of the hotel and typed the interstate into his GPS. He drove away from Cooney's Corners, Brigit de Ville, and after a while he saw signs indicating the road he was on was intersecting with I-10, next turn west, east intersection second exit. He began to turn his steering wheel so that he could continue west and home, then at the last second continued driving straight until he saw the east interstate arrow. He turned and was headed back toward Baton Rouge. It had begun to rain.

When he entered the city he took the first exit into the city. He had to stop at three service stations before he found one that had a telephone book. He looked through the yellow pages for Catholic churches. Peter remembered that they were always presided over by priests. Maybe non-Catholic clergy did them, but he was not sure. He was not going to take a chance. Not being very religious he didn't know there would be several in Baton Rouge. He wrote down several addresses after he decided which ones would be the larger. He put the first address into his GPS and drove to it. He parked, got out of his car and entered the church. Never had he been in a Catholic church so when he saw the interior he was impressed and was sure he had made the correct decision to come here. The church was huge with a high ceiling, supported by half walls supported with columns. Between the columns and recessed was an extension of the church with a much lower ceiling its walls were made up of a series of stained-glass windows and between the windows were a series of portraits of saints. At the front of the church was a raised platform and on it was what he assumed was an altar, a podium and behind it, a huge stained-glass window. When he entered the church on one side he saw a number of glasses with candles in them, some were lit. Peter saw three people sitting in pews and a person, he assumed was a custodian, cleaning the seating area and he went to him. "I need to see the priest. How can I do it? Can you help me?"

The custodian looked at him and said, "Wait here I'll get him." The man left through a side door and soon returned with a priest.

When they returned to Peter, he saw a middle-aged man, Peter guessed in his mid to late forties. He was dressed like all the priests Peter had seen on TV or in the movies, in black with a white collar. When the two men reached Peter, they stopped, the custodian turned around and went back cleaning the seating area. The priest stuck out his hand to shake Peter's hand and asked, "What can I do for you my son?" Peter was silent, he didn't know how he was going to explain what he needed. "Do you wish to make a confession?" the priest continued.

Peter wasn't quite sure how to begin but he asked, "How do I address you?"

The priest smiled and answered, "Call me Father Lonnie, short for Lonniston, or just Father."

"I need your help. I need someone to talk to about being possessed by spirits, witches and the devil." From what Peter knew about exorcisms, they had always been performed by priests and if anyone knew about witches, it would be a priest. He had decided this would be his best course of action.

The priest invited Peter to sit on a pew, paused, and sat beside him before he asked, "Do you believe that you are possessed? Know someone who is? Seen a body occupied by the devil?" When he didn't get an immediate answer he hesitated before he asked another question, "Have you seen the devil, an evil spirt? Know someone who has?"

"Yes," Peter finally replied. "I've seen a witch, seen the devil." They were both silent for a moment.

"The witch, did she cast a spell? You want to break the spell, it, destroy her?" Peter remained silent. Finally, Father Lonniston asked, "Did you see this witch, sorceress, in a house, on the street or in a rural setting?" Peter just shook his head yes, not telling the priest exactly where he saw Sofianna. The priest smiled at Peter but with a note of seriousness followed up with a question, "Did you see her in New Orleans, here in Baton Rouge or in the country?"

Peter didn't answer him but was shaking his head up and down and mumbled, "Yes."

"Haitian voodoo priestesses are everywhere down here. I wouldn't put much stock in anything they may say or do. They are not Christian. The work of the devil," then he was silent. After a long pause, he said, "You strike me as an intelligent young man, educated. You need to know the church doesn't openly condone anything like that, a witch trial. They are done occasionally by some rural priests. It's all Hollywood. If a person is possessed, believes he or she is a witch it normally is only in their mind and they are able to convince those around them. There are priests who condemn them in the name of God, do exorcisms once in a while, but for the most part they are not acknowledged by the church, although in some countries it is a common practice, especially in Haiti and some European countries."

"And if you believe that you have seen the devil? Seen a witch dance with the devil" Peter replied.

"There is no such thing as a witch, a sorceress, someone in league with the devil. Was this witch part of a group, at night around a fire so that the devil was not clearly seen? It came and went at her command?"

Peter listened to the priest and didn't say anything, "A voodoo priestess cannot call or demand the devil to appear, be at her command." When Peter did not respond, the priest added, "The bishop's position is just that, you believed that you saw a witch, the devil, you or a friend are possessed by him or a demon. There is no proof that it happened. What you saw was a show, either to frighten the onlookers and/or to give the witch/sorcerer more notoriety." Father Lonniston said. "Or you imagined it. If it didn't happen, was real, how can it condemned, be exorcised? But, if you believe that the devil has been exorcised, then maybe he has been."

Peter thought about what he was just told. It was very similar to his not believing there was anything to witches, that they existed. How can one help you if witches don't exist? But they do. He had seen and talked to one, one who was in league with the devil, and he had seen the devil. He was silent for a while, not going to get any help from the priest.

He asked, "What if I wanted to get more information about evil spirits, witches and the devil, where would I find it. Is there someone I could talk to? A book I should read?"

"Why do you have an interest in such things?" the priest asked. "The things you talk about are the work of the devil. If you want to know more, read the bible."

"I'm curious, I want to know more," and then Peter lied, "I'm thinking of writing a book on the devil, spirits, good and bad, and exorcisms."

"The church is not in the movie business. I can't help you son. Like Hollywood, you will have to make it up," Father Lonniston told him.

Peter would not give up. "If I wanted to kill the devil, how would I do it? Can it be done?"

The priest looked at him with a bit of a smile on his face. "If you believe that the Catholic church knows how to kill the devil, don't you think that they would have done it hundreds of years ago? He can't be killed. This is life, not a movie where a priest can kill the devil. The earth is his. What he sees, he wants, he takes. Can't be stopped. Ask God for help and guidance. He is the only one who can and will help you. You need faith. You cannot do it on your own, you have to have God's help."

This was the second time that Peter had heard about the earth being the devil's. He was not pleased with what he heard and it was obvious. He did not know what else to say or ask. Father Lonniston could see the disappointment on Peter's face. "I can't help you, but there is someone you should talk to, a Cajun priest, Father Thibodeaux. He's the oldest priest in our diocese. I believe that he is ninety-three years old. He believes in exorcisms and to satisfy some of his mixed Haitian and Cajun flock, it is said that he will occasionally perform one. Haven't heard of him condemning a witch for a while though, they seem to have fallen out of favor even though a lot of people down there believe in evil spirits, people being possessed, witches. Church cannot make them believe otherwise. He believes that if a person believes he or she is possessed, an exorcism will then cause him to believe that he has been helped. The church doesn't condone it but overlook his performing the ritual. It keeps those in his church pleased. He could shed some light on what you wish to know, give you some details. Maybe explain why he does exorcisms, how he does them and the results. Maybe why few people believe in sorceresses. How successful he is. How the exorcised person responds, how an accused witch responds. How the person he helped lives afterward. Do they become devout Christians, believing in God?"

"And what does he say about witches?"

"I've heard that he tries to steer his congregate away from believing in them. They are the work of the devil, will lead man astray. Need to be ignored. The bible often talks about them, that they should be cast aside. In the bible they are to be stoned. Stoned in the bible means only one thing, killed."

After Peter heard everything Father Lonniston said, he believed Father Thibodeaux was the priest Peter should see. "Where can I find him?" he asked.

"He's a priest in Terrebonne Parish, ministers near the gulf. You may have to have someone take you to see him in a boat. It has been a wet year and southern Terrebonne is real bayou country, few roads. A lot of them are considered back roads, are dirt or mud and not on any map," Father Lonniston told him, "easy to get lost. Or worse, drive into the swamp, never be heard of or seen again. I wouldn't try it if I were you. There's nothing more I can tell you or help with. I wish you luck in your search."

Peter thanked him for his time and patience. Everywhere seems to be real bayou country. He wasn't sure exactly what that meant. He left the church and went to his car. He wondered if he should leave, head back to Colorado or continue to look for a solution to Sofianna's problem and ultimately what was plaguing him, his dreams, his nightmares. Could he have Sofianna break her pact with the devil, help her and satisfy her spell on him and herself, that someone would help her.

He knew why his nightmares occurred so he could deal with them. The more he thought about the situation, the stronger his determination became to fix both, her dance with the devil and his dreams had to be able to be resolved. He would have to find an answer. He would look for a priest who could help him.

When he got in his car it was already late in the afternoon, so he decided to stay in Baton Rouge for the night. Before he left the church's parking lot he began to type into his GPS, Terrebonne parish. He only typed in 'TE' when he realized he did not know how to spell it. He touched the speak button and said the name. Immediately his GPS told him where to turn when he left the parking lot, instead of driving to Terrebonne parish, he began to look for a hotel.

Chapter 14

❧

That night in his hotel room Peter got a map of Louisiana to see exactly where Terrebonne Parish was. Satisfied he went to sleep and would start out tomorrow. Once he got to the parish he would use his GPS to locate catholic churches in the area and then seek Father Thibodeaux. That night he dreamed, not of a dreadful situation, or a blonde who reminded him of his neighbor, but how to help the woman in his dreams who needed his help, who now had a name, Sofianna. That night there was only the silent pleas from his dream woman.

After he had a quick breakfast he began driving to his new destination. When he crossed the parish line he got off the interstate and began to look for a town. He found one and typed into his GPS Catholic churches. None. He stopped a young man and asked for the nearest Catholic church. He was told it was near the high school which was near the post office. Peter obviously had a blank stare on his face when the young man realized that Peter didn't know where any of the buildings were that had been referred to. He was given directions, thanked the young man, drove to it and entered. It was quite different from the one in Baton Rouge. It resembled it but had a much more of a spartan feel. At what would be the altar he saw the priest. He was an older overweight man. Peter walked to him. "Father, I'm Peter Frost. I'm searching for Father Thibodeaux; can you help me? Tell me where I might be able to find him, his church?"

The priest studied Peter for a moment, stuck out his hand to shake Peter's hand and with a big smile on his face said, "I'm Father Degan. Of course, but I doubt you will be able to find his church or him. It's close to the gulf and he travels between two churches."

"Can I drive to there and look for his church?" Peter asked.

"Yes, but I wouldn't advise it unless you drive a four-wheel SUV, know the bayou and roads. It has been raining and the roads are not in the best condition and many are unmarked. Plus, Lake Boudeaux is high. The area is real bayou country."

"I need to talk to him. Can you help me?"

The priest looked at him for a moment before he responded, "If you really need to find him, I suggest you drive to Houma and hire a guide with a boat to take you there. It's going to cost you. But, if you are determined I can give you the names of two gator hunters, honest and can be trusted. Should be able to guide you. Most likely might cost you close to fifty dollars a day, gas, the guide's food and possible lodging if you have to spend the night somewhere."

Peter didn't ask the priest where, in this real bayou country, there would be a motel or hotel, nor did he tell Father Degan why he wished to see Father Thibodeaux. He thanked the priest and using his GPS drove to Houma and found Rodney, no last name, one of the gator hunters Father Degan told him about. Again, using his GPS found Rodney's address which was near the water, even though it wasn't displayed on a mailbox or his house. Peter didn't know if this was the lake the priest told him about. He made a deal with Rodney and found that he fished, hunted alligators, and logged occasionally. He was a muscular man who smoked and needed a shave. He wouldn't smoke around Peter, but he would have an unlit cigarette dangling from the corner of his mouth. Rodney told him he would take Peter by boat to find the priest, Father Thibodeaux, regardless which of the two churches he ministered to. It would cost Peter fifty dollars a day or any part of a day. Had Father Degan called him? Told him about Peter? Peter didn't know or spend any time thinking about it. The round trip would most likely take one day if the priest were at the nearest of the two churches he ministered to. Two days if they would need to go to the gulf.

The next morning it was cloudy when they set out with a cooler, Rodney said his woman, who Peter never met, had packed sandwiches for them, a large thermos of coffee and a five-gallon container of gas. Rodney told Peter that the last thing they would want to happen was run out of gas miles from nowhere. When they started, the first thing Peter noticed was the smell of the swamp. Now every time Peter was to smell the swamp he would associate the smell with the devil, the smell of evil. It wasn't as strong as when he went to Sofianna's, but the smell was present. He commented on it and Rodney told him it is the decaying vegetation and stagnant water, just as he thought. It would be a lot less when they reached the lake. Peter thought that maybe Rodney should light the cigarette he had hanging in his mouth, it could mask the swamp smell.

After several twists and turns into different channels of water they soon came upon a large body of water. "Lake Boudreaux," was all that he heard Rodney say. "Now we make good time, be there no time." Rodney's house had not been on the lake. Either he had become used to the smell or what Rodney had said was true. Peter could not smell the swamp at all.

Peter believed he would never have been able to find his way to the priest considering the twists and turns Rodney made with the boat before they arrived at the lake. Peter hoped that Rodney was taking him where he wanted to go and was not just sailing around, taking longer to reach the priest so that he could get more money from this guy from the city. It had only been half an hour since they left Houma when it became windy and began to rain. It seemed that wind gusts lifted sheets of water from the lake and blew the water toward them. The rain dissolved Rodney's cigarette and it disappeared, but he kept the filter in his mouth. Rodney slowed down and in a matter of seconds they were both soaking wet. Peter believed that he couldn't see a hundred feet ahead of him. He was unable to see a shoreline or trees. He hoped Rodney knew where he was going. After several minutes Rodney turned the boat to his right and slowed down. Through the rain Peter could see a rough looking dock that extended into the water. Rodney eased the boat alongside it, stopped, put both the cooler and thermos on the dock and jumped out. He asked Peter to pick up the rope at the front of the boat and told him to tie the boat to the dock. Then Rodney told Peter, "Come on," as he stepped out of the boat. Peter could see in the distance a house on close to six-foot-high concrete block stilts. Was this the church area the priest Peter was looking for, ministered to? Could it be this small? Was it close? It hadn't taken so long to reach it. Instead, Rodney said, "We stop here for a while, my friend Averell's place. Dry out and continue later if rain stops. Maybe eat a sandwich or two." Peter saw him spit out the cigarette filter.

They climbed the stairs to the house Rodney knocked on the door and it opened. "This my friend Averell," Rodney said to Peter and then he said to Averell, "this Peter Frost, taking him to meet up with Father Thibodeaux," and the two men shook hands. "Need to get out of the rain and dry out. Hope you don't mind." Averell was almost the opposite of Rodney, slight build and clean shaven. "You're more than welcome friend, heard your boat. Wondered who'd be out in dis weather. Take off your clothes. I'll throw dem in the dryer." Peter never asked or wondered how this out of the way house was supplied with electricity. He thought it better not to ask. "I'll get two blankets for you. Martha's on da Mississippi with mom and pop. Why no boat at dock."

For the next hour, as their clothes dried, Rodney and Averell talked about fishing and hunting alligators, especially Crooked Tooth. This was a very large alligator that had a crooked tooth in the front, lived in the lake or one of its various channels that led to the lake, was difficult to get close to and able to avoid their baited traps. As the two men discussed what they might try to get the gator, Peter could hear the rain hit the roof of the house. He believed it was going to be an all-day rain. Then the conversation turned to Peter. "Why you want see Father Thibodeaux?" Averell asked.

Peter said, "I want to know more about witches and exorcisms and heard from a priest in Baton Rouge, he would be the person to talk to.

Think I need one for Sofianna, a friend of mine. She believes she is a witch and needs to be exorcised. I want to know more about witches, her, and her past. What has led her to this belief, what possesses her, can she be exorcised, made to believe that she is not a witch."

"He sure 'nough do them once a while. Can tell you. He Martha's priest. Tell a secret. You want to get him talking take a pint of bourbon wit you. Share it wit him. He talk then. Like to be lubricated," Averell said with a slight chuckle.

Peter thought it might be a good idea, but where was he going to buy something like that. There were no stores here in the real bayou country. Peter saw the two men smile at each other when he asked, "Where can I but something like that around here?"

"Can't," Peter heard his guide Rodney say. "Have to go all the way back to Houma." When Peter heard this, he had a disappointed look on his face. Rodney came to his rescue, "You wouldn't have any you might be willing to sell, would you Averell?" was the next question that came from Rodney.

"Well," and he paused. He scratched his chin as if thinking before he continued, "I just might," Averell said.

Peter thought to himself that he was from the city and was about to be taken advantage of by these two back-woods hillbillies. He thought it safe to be prepared however, and if it meant that he had to pay an outrageous price for a bottle of liquor, so be it. "Would you be willing to sell it?" asked Rodney.

Peter waited and wondered if Averell would be willing to sell it? After a moment he finally asked, "What would it cost me to buy it from you?"

Averell continued to scratch his chin as he thought about what he had been asked. Would he sell it? Or was he thinking what he could ask for it and get from Peter.

Finally, he said, "Well, let's see. First, I wouldn't be able to have my customary before bed drink, then I'd have to gas up my boat, then get in my boat and go all the way to Houma, miss a day's work. I don't rightly know," Averell said. Peter had not heard from either Rodney or Averell that Averell had any sort of a job. He was about ready to say something to that fact, thought better of it, and kept quiet. Better to just buy the bourbon from Averell. If it was to be an outrageous price, so be it. He would pay it.

Rodney spoke up for him, "I think thirty dollars would do it, don't you think so Averell?"

He continued to scratch his chin as if he were giving the suggested price serious thought. "Yeah. That ough'ta do it," he replied.

Peter didn't think that it was an outrageous price. Rodney was on Peter's side. Peter went to where he placed his wallet and opened it. He took out a wet twenty and a ten and paid him. Averell went into the cupboard above the sink and got the three-quarters full pint bottle of bourbon. While they were talking Peter hadn't noticed that the rain had stopped. Rodney went to a window, looked out and said, "Looks like the storm is almost over, just a squall from the gulf. Sun is trying to break through. It's mid-afternoon and if we're goin to reach his church before dark, better git goin."

After an hour Peter and Rodney got dressed and were ready to leave when Averell said, "Don't directly offer the priest a drink, but ask if it would be okay if you had one. Pour it and ask if you can pour one also for him," and handed the bottle to Peter and gave him a big smile.

Peter wondered if what this alligator hunter had told him was the truth or was he playing a joke on him, a joke that he and Rodney would share and laugh at in the future.

"I'll return this," and Rodney held up a towel. Rodney loaded their cooler and thermos into the boat, wiped off their seats, bailed out rainwater as best as he could, placed a cigarette in his mouth and they set out. Peter didn't ask where Rodney had gotten a dry cigarette. The sun did shine, and Peter saw several houses on stilts close to the water. After a short time, Rodney steered the boat to a wooden dock, got out and told Peter to wait in the boat. Rodney went to one of the houses. He came back shortly and told Peter the priest was at his furthest church, beyond the lake in Cokodrie. "Cokodrie is just several houses close to each other," Rodney said, "and you would never been able to find it because it was not on any map." They continued their journey and eventually made it off the lake and up several side channels before they reached Cokodrie just as the sun was about to set. Rodney led Peter to the church. It was a lot smaller than the two Peter had been in, but it did have some of the same trappings and Peter recognized it as a church. He met and was introduced to Father Thibodeaux. Like he was told by Father Lonniston, Thibodeaux looked like he was ninety-three. He used a cane when he walked but after they began to talk, Peter thought he was a spry ninety-three old man. He was thin and looked a bit pasty. After introductions Rodney excused himself and told Peter he would be in the local bar. Peter later was to find out that Cokodrie may have consisted of several houses with no stores or shops, but it did have a local bar, or what would pass for a bar. Before he left, Rodney tipped his hand up as if taking a drink from a bottle for Peter to see. Peter remembered what Averell had said about a drink. The body of the priest may have been old but not his mind. As they began to talk Peter realized that the old priest was sharp. They sat in a church pew. "What can I do for you my son," the elderly priest asked.

Peter was not sure where to begin. "It has been a long and wet day, came all the way from Houma. Forgive me for saying, but I need a drink. If it offends you I will go outside," and he pulled the pint bottle from his pocket.

"Not at all," Father Thibodeaux said, "in fact I have a wee nip or two myself occasionally, specially on these chilly damp days, help keep the chill-banes away." Peter never asked if he wanted a drink, he unscrewed the lid, feigned taking a drink and passed the bottle to the priest. He watched him take two big drinks before he passed the bottle back to Peter. "Now, what were we talking about?"

Peter decided to get right to the point. "Tell me about witches, exorcisms."

The priest looked at Peter and said, "There is no such thing as a witch and the church doesn't always approve of exorcisms, we don't do them." Both were silent for a moment before Thibodeaux asked, "Did the Bishop send you?"

"No. Father Lonniston of Baton Rouge did. He told me if I wanted to know more about witches I should see you and you still performed exorcisms."

When the priest hesitated to answer, Peter held out the pint bottle of bourbon to him. The priest took it, unscrewed the lid, and took a large drink. He handed the bottle back to Peter and asked, "Why you want to know bout them? Know someone who believe they are possessed?"

Peter thought to himself that maybe what Averell had said about the priest being talkative after a drink or two was true. He said, "I know someone, a friend, a witch, who is visited by the devil. I've seen him. I want to know what I can do to stop him. Do I need a priest?"

"You are serious, aren't you, believe your friend is a witch and you have seen the devil." Father Thibodeaux said. "Most people are determined that the devil possesses them, makes them do things, unnatural things. But you say that you've actually seen the devil?" he asked.

All Peter could say was, "Yes."

"Tell me about it, what you believe you saw," Father Thibodeaux said.

For the next ten minutes Peter described what he had seen at Sofianna's cabin on the night of the dark of the moon, her dance with the evil spirits and finally with the devil. Peter said nothing about his dreams, of Sofianna accidently calling to him. He saw the priest look away from him and close his eyes. When Peter finished talking, he said, "What you say you saw is the first time someone has come to me to tell of such an experience. I believe you. What you saw was most likely one of Satan's angels and not the devil himself. She is not possessed. Can't exorcise him. He doesn't possess her body nor can she summon him. Sounds more like a long time ago she made a deal with him and he comes to her to collect." The priest allowed Peter to think about what he said before he said, "What would you like to do?"

"Stop him, maybe kill him," Peter answered.

"He is part of the earth, can't be killed. All that can be done is send him back to hell and leave your friend alone," the priest replied.

"How can I do that? Can you do it? If I pay you, will you come with me and do it?"

"No. I will not go with you. I would be unable to stop him. It is questionable if it can be done, send the angel back to hell. I've never been asked to do that, stop something evil from visiting a person. Others may have been asked to do so, but not me. I've only dealt with evil demons who possess a person. He will not stop. Satan's angels are like men with the same weaknesses. He saw her, wanted her and she made a bargain with him. Gave her powers and in return he demanded a child, a male child. He will have to release her from their bargain or, she must do what he wants. He is persistent and patient. Will wait a lifetime. Will have her."

"At her age is that possible? Can she get pregnant?"

"If he is able to make her young on the outside then also on the inside. So yes, she can become with child. It is believed by some in the church that from the beginning of time the most vile, evil men ever were the sons of the devil. Somewhere, somehow a woman prayed to Satan, worshipped him and one of his angels heard her pleas, went to her. Or one of Satan's angels saw a beautiful woman and took a fancy to the woman. That is what has happened to your friend. Maybe the angel saw her, wanted her and she made a bargain with the angel, not for her soul but for some earthly powers, she would give the angel what she bargained for, a son. You said she is a witch. She most likely was one already and he gave her the limited ability to be a more powerful one. All she needed to do was give the angel a son, a son who then would be handed off to the angel's master, Satan. With other women, if he couldn't make a bargain with them, he would take the place of a husband or lover and get the woman with child, a male child. She would not know. When these children, the spawn of evil grew up, they would be very susceptible to what Satan wanted done, easily influenced by Satan to become powerful men and to do evil on earth, do evil to their fellow man. There are very few who believe the way I do. I may be one of the last. Your story of the witch and the devil validates what I have believed for years. If I were younger I would go with you, see it for myself. But I'm too old now, couldn't even do a decent job writing about it. Make it believable."

"Help me. What can I do?" Peter asked.

"I don't know. Let me pray and think about it tonight. Come back tomorrow," the priest said as he looked at the almost empty bottle of bourbon.

Peter didn't say anything more. The priest believed him. He got up and turned to leave the church. Peter left the bottle with bourbon.

Outside it was dark, but he was able to find the local bar. A few of the houses had lights but the neon sign in the bar stood out. Lit up in its window was a beer, a name he didn't recognize, being poured into a glass. When he opened the door, if what he saw was a bar, this was it. In a smoke-filled room poorly lit he saw three men talking and drinking beer from glasses, one was Rodney. Several thick pieces of lumber, two or three 2x12's edge to edge and twelve feet or longer in length were supported by what Peter believed were custom built sawhorses. The pieces of lumber, nicked and burned with several ash trays, served as a counter. Of the ten stools at it, there were only four that matched, three were cushioned and two that had backs. Directly behind the counter in a separate room was what served as the kitchen/cooking area with an opening that served as a food pass-through similar to the one at Cooney's Corner. To one side he could see only five different types of hard liquor, glasses, and a small sink. A beer tap at that end of the counter had a hose that ran to one of two refrigerators that were beneath the counter. On both sides of the pass-through opening were a number of different beer logos and a second one that was lit in the place's window. Also to one side was a menu written in chalk, again similar to the restaurant at Cooney's Corner, beneath, not written in chalk was the place's name, Pete's Tavern. If he wanted a beer it would be a draft from the tap or one of only two brands the tavern had, the one advertised in the window, in a bottle or a can that came from the second refrigerator beneath the counter. There were no booths. Five tables had an assortment of different chairs at them. In a corner of the room was a small bumper pool table and a dart board on the wall. These last two items finished off the room. This time Rodney had a lit cigarette in his mouth.

Peter went to Rodney and told him they would have to spend the night, Peter would have to see the priest tomorrow, which was okay with Rodney. Before he could ask where he might find a place to stay, Peter was told about a seedy room off the kitchen that had a cot, he could stay there. Peter said to the bar tender/owner, a short stocky man of about fifty, "This my friend Peter I tell you about." The bar tender said his name was Pete and he owned this establishment, shook Peter's hand and led him through and beyond the kitchen to the room. It was dirty and unkempt and served as a storeroom and looked like the floor hadn't been swept for months but he needed to stay somewhere so he said okay to the room. There would be no charge. Peter never asked where Rodney would stay and when he and Pete returned to the bar, Rodney was gone. Before he turned in Peter ordered a hamburger and a beer, a brand he recognized, Coors. Pete walked to the end of the bar and through the door opening they both had just walked through to the kitchen. Peter could smell meat cooking and after several minutes Pete brought both to Peter. When Peter went to the back room all that he could do was shake out the sheets and inspect the mattress for any type of bug that might be there. He decided to keep his clothes on when he went to sleep.

The next morning when he woke he found his way to the bathroom, off the kitchen, splashed water on his face and ran his fingers through his hair. When he walked into the bar Peter was not surprised to see people there, eating or drinking. Rodney was at a table, invited Peter to join him and took out of a paper bag two cups of coffee with lids on them and what looked like homemade egg McMuffins. Again, Peter never asked Rodney where he got their breakfast, he just ate his and drank the coffee. After they finished, Rodney went to the counter and ordered a beer from the woman working. Rodney told Peter the woman was Pete's wife, never said her name, and when Peter was ready to leave she gladly sold him a half full bottle of bourbon. Before he left Rodney told Peter when he was ready to leave he could find him in the bar. Peter headed to the church to meet with the priest. As he was leaving he saw Rodney put a cigarette in his mouth.

Peter entered Father Thibodeaux's church and sat at a pew and waited. He dozed off while he waited, and he felt himself being shaken awake by Father Thibodeaux. The priest handed Peter a white bed sheet. "I thought about what you said and I prayed most of the night, sought guidance. I asked God if I could, should go with you. I didn't get an answer, so I will not go with you."

Peter was disappointed but it was the same answer the priest gave him yesterday. He looked at the sheet given to him and wondered why a sheet.

Before he could ask about it Father Thibodeaux said, "All I could come up with is this sheet. It has been washed in holy water and has a cross sewn into the top. If you want it to work, it will be necessary for you to draw a cross on it with the blood of one of her descendants, since he wants her to produce a son for him, he will not cross it. Cover her with it and he won't be able to see her. What he can't see, he can't covet. The reason his minions, his demons, they are not spirits, bring her out. He cannot see her in her cabin and for some reason he won't enter her cabin."

Peter took the sheet and asked, "Will it work?"

"It might. After a night of prayer, it is all that I could come up with," Father Thibodeaux said. He ended the conversation by telling Peter, "Good luck," and he got up but before he could leave Peter offered him the bottle he bought at the bar. He thanked Peter and walked to the front of the church. Peter was unable to ask or say anything else and he could see the priest kneeling and it looked like praying. Peter hoped the prayer was for him and his quest. If it worked Peter promised himself that he would send the priest a case of bourbon.

Peter found Rodney and told him that they should return to Houma. During the return trip Peter wondered what he should do next. If he needed blood from one of Sofianna's descendants, that would, should be the next move, but he had not heard of her having children, being married. He just assumed that she was not married or had children.

Peter felt the pain of disappointment. Had he reached a dead end? Yes. Would he give up on trying to help Sofianna? Yes. Was there anything that he could do? No.

Chapter 15

Rodney took Peter back to Houma where he looked at his map of Louisiana and found Lake De Cade. He was surprised how close it was to Houma. If that was where Sofianna was from, maybe she has family members there. They might be able to shed some light about her past. Maybe he could find them. Thinking optimistically, he expected to find relatives. Except for Father Thibodeau, he never talked about the pact with the angel from hell, and when he found Sofianna's relatives he wouldn't need to mention it. Was it possible that she had children prior to her pact? He wanted to find some of Sofianna's family and more of her history. He talked to Rodney about it. "Could the lake area be reached from Houma?"

The answer from Rodney was, "Yes."

Peter next told Rodney what he needed to do, locate any of the Brecht family who may have been alive well over sixty, seventy years ago. Was Brecht her last name? Peter was not sure; he had never asked anyone and was never told. He only assumed it was Brecht because she claimed to be related to the Brecht brothers.

Because Peter did not know where they might live or have lived, Rodney suggested, "They may not be on the lake but in the general area. I will be more than happy to travel to Lake De Cade and search for them at fifty dollars a day plus expenses, the same cost per day as when we searched for Father Thibodeau. I don't know how many people I will have to talk to." Peter agreed and he would stay in a motel just outside of Houma.

It was three days later when Rodney returned. He was unable to locate any Brechts, but was able to find several Albrecht families, one family would have been old enough to have lived in the area of the lake around the time when the woman Peter wanted to know more about had lived. Peter believed it would be worth his time to talk to them. Easy for an Albrecht to leave the "A" off their name. Rodney said the two oldest family members he talked to were alive sixty or more years ago. All the other Albrechts were too young to have known the woman. In addition, he added that they were heavy smokers, and it might be worth taking along a couple of cartons of cigarettes with them to use as incentives to get them to talk. Rodney's friend Averell knew what would be necessary to get the priest into a talkative mood and Peter agreed. This man from the bayous had a real feel and understanding of the people he lived among. Peter thought it a good idea and if the cigarettes wouldn't work on the Albrechts, he was sure Rodney would be glad to take the two cartons of cigarettes.

Peter was taken by boat to the northwestern side of the lake to meet the two Albrecht family members Rodney had told him about. The home of the family he met was on high ground near the lake and when he and Rodney went to the door, carved into the door was the symbol. When Peter saw it, his spirits soared. By luck, the family he would talk to was the correct family. The family consisted of the old man and woman and there were their children, two men and a woman. It appeared that they all lived in the same house. After introductions Peter asked if they were related to or knew the Brecht brothers who moved to Brigit de Ville. Gram Paul was the oldest looking of the family Peter talked to. He looked to be a hundred, tanned and weathered, gray beard, almost bald and smoked a pipe. "Yep," was the old man's answer. "Dey famy. Both ded. Change name, not wan be lated to da witch."

Peter was delighted when he heard someone in the family was a witch. He asked, "You mean Sofianna?"

"Yep," the old man replied grinning as he blew out smoke.

Peter decided to take a chance when he said, "I know her. Can you tell me about her?"

Before Gram Paul could answer, the old woman, Grammie Mattie, looked the same age, missing two of her front lower teeth, gray hair also smoking a pipe and he believed was Gram Paul's wife muttered, "A hum, a hum." Peter could see that she had good top teeth. He thought maybe they were false. At Peter's request she spoke, "Knew Sofia special when bout ten, leven. Had de giff. Fortens, spells an stuff. Kin folk fraid er. Stay way. Fore all these chillens," and she waved her hand to include the others in the room. "What you wanna know?"

Rodney who was quiet during the conversation took out of his backpack a carton of cigarettes. When he did, all the family smiled. He held the carton out to Grammie Mattie and said, "Yours if'n you tell him bout er."

With a big smile that hid her missing teeth, Grammie Mattie was quick to answer, "Born wiff giff. Sixeen, seveneen cast spell on neibor boy Avery. They marry up. Did'n las."

"Year, two, maybe more later, he lev her and babe Dannell," added Gram Paul.

Peter waited for more and as soon as Grammie Mattie exhaled, she replied, "Doon know where he go. Nev hear see Avery gain."

Gram Paul answered fo her, "She up and go, coupa years. Up north somewhere, ten to Brigit de Ville. Fer as know, she still dere."

Peter had a spark of hope when he asked, "What happened to Daniel? Is he around?"

"No," Grammie Mattie answered. "Aft'a bout two-year, Auntie Milly tak babe up da riber ta Memphis."

"Did she change her name?" Peter asked.

"No. Hear bot ded. Lived on da riber, she drown," Grammie Mattie said.

Peter was not happy to hear the last statement. It sounded like he would not be able to find any of Sofianna's decedents, there were none.

She had had a son but now he was dead, or was he? "Did Daniel drown too?"

"Tink so," Grammie Mattie said. "Don know fer sure. Nev here from em."

Peter thanked the Albrechts for their time, told Rodney to give them the two cartons of cigarettes and prepared to leave. He stopped and turned to them, each with a carton of cigarettes and smiling. "Two last questions. Did Sofianna have green eyes?"

"Yep," replied Grammie Mattie. "Fam'ly taught debil eyes. See trew youse. More prouf she had giff. People 'lieve her Ma lay wit da debil. Sofianna da spawn of da debil. Mos fraid of er. Stay way."

"What else wanna know?" asked Gram Paul.

"What is the purpose of the symbol carved into your door? Does it have a meaning?"

Gram Paul smiled at him and replied, "To keep debil out. Bless by priest, splash holy water on it. Will not cross pas it, come fer us night."

He again thanked them and thought that Ms. Schwarz's friend saying it was a devil worship cult symbol was wrong. It was the reason the Brecht brothers carved it in their doors.

He and Rodney returned to Houma. He wrote a check made out to one name, Rodney, for all that he did for him, it was a lot less than what he had paid Ms. Schwarz, the dream center and what his trip to Florida cost. And of all the things he had tried, this adventure gave him real results. What to do next? Return to Denver and learn to live with his dreams? No. Drive to Memphis. Search for Daniel he thought.

Chapter 16

He saw the sign, Memphis next five exits. Sometime during his trip to the Albrecht's, Peter had become fixated with following the trail of Sofianna and the reason for his desperate nightmares. Or maybe it was the idea of helping Sofianna. Peter was not sure of which. It didn't matter.

He decided to make sure that Auntie Milly and Daniel were both dead. He called Justine and told her he would not return for another week or so. He wouldn't permit her to ask any questions and gave her no details. After he checked into a hotel he found the local library and on its computer he found nothing of a Milly Albrecht. Was it possible that she had changed her name? No. The Albrechts at Lake De Cade never said anything about Auntie Milly changing her name like the Brecht brothers. Next, he began to look for past deaths in the city. The records only went back one year. The librarian suggested he look at older newspaper notices of city deaths. Peter found that the local newspaper went back to its beginning before the turn of the twentieth century and had put all its past editions on computer. He began searching old newspaper obituaries. Did Auntie Milly live in Memphis or near the city? He did not ask either of the Albrechts nor did he know how long ago she moved. Peter didn't know when or where to begin looking. There were several newspapers in or near the city. He took a guess that he would start his search eighty years ago.

After three days of diligently searching, Peter found it. The obituary for Mildred (Milly) Albrecht, she was drowned in the 1947 flood. She was survived by her son Dannell and his wife, Sheri. He believed when the Albrechts said Sofianna had a son, Dannell, they slurred the name Daniel or Sofianna had misspelled it on his birth certificate. If Peter tried to look up Daniel he would have had trouble. He had no idea how his name, Dannell, was spelled, but now he knew. After Auntie Milly moved to Memphis she claimed Dannell as her son. No one ever checked on the validity of her claim. Why would they? Why didn't she change Dannell's name? Why should she? She wouldn't know about Sofianna's pact with the angel from hell. All she was sure of was that Sofianna's husband had disappeared. Then she would have known that Sofianna had abandoned her son. There was no further information concerning either. Additional searching turned up nothing. He could find nothing on Dannell Albrecht. He began to look at marriage applications prior to 1937. Two days later he found it. A license to marry was reported in the paper for Sheri White to Dannell Albrecht.

Where to look next? In the Memphis and surrounding area there were several Whites. He began calling them, one at a time. He identified himself as a lawyer and a Mr. Dannell Albrecht may have come into a sizeable amount of money. It would now possibly go to him or his heirs. Did the Whites he talked to have a daughter, or a granddaughter named Sheri, maybe a cousin, a relative who would have married Mr. Albrecht? On the fifth call a woman said her daughter married Dannell. Peter wanted to know how he could get in touch with her or Dannell. "He dead," was the answer Peter received.

"What about Sheri?" he asked.

"After his mother Milly died, Dannell, Sheri, and my daughter Bell, all move to Cleveland after my husband, Sam, died, Sheri and Bell's father. Never did get along, maybe for the best. Don't know where. Get a phone call every so often or a letter from Bell once in a while, no return address. Bell tells me once I was now a grandmother, Sheri had a baby girl, called her Candice. Then three, maybe four year later get a letter, tell me Dannell died. Car wreck. Not where, just died. She quit writing or calling. Not heard from her again. Couldn't tell her or Sheri, their father died."

Another dead end. What to do? Should he return to Denver? No. So close he would keep looking. Cleveland would be his next stop. Sofianna had descents and he had to find them if he were to get the sheet to work.

Chapter 17

When Peter decided to drive to Cleveland, he had no idea how large the city was or its population. He booked a room in a hotel and looked in a current telephone book in the room for Albrecht. He found no Sheri or Candice with that last name. In this day and age, it would not be unusual for them to not be listed. He again began to search the obituaries for Dannell, same results, wasn't listed. The second day of looking made him tired. That night when he went to sleep he thought, why not get someone else to do the looking for him. If he were home, he would have one or both of his assistants do it.

When he arose, he went to the telephone book in his hotel room and looked up private investigators. He found several who specialized in surveillance. One did not specialize. No request too big or too small caught his eye. Call R. Dix Investigations. He called the number and made an appointment with a receptionist to see the investigator. He was surprised and believed that he had made a mistake when the investigator turned out to be a woman. Her name was Ruby Dix. She was the same age as Ms. Schwarz, mousey brown curly hair, brown eyes, smartly dressed in a pants suit and had an air of confidence about her that he liked. After she invited him into her office and he was seated she asked if she could get him a cup of coffee, a water? He shook his head yes, "I'll have a cup of coffee, black."

Ms. Dix picked up her phone and gave her receptionist Peter's request. While they waited she began to tell him of her qualifications before she asked him what he wanted her to do. "I graduated from OSU with a degree in criminal justice. I spent a year in law school when I discovered lawyering was not for me. I dropped out, applied for detective training, and then worked as a detective on the Cleveland police force for over fifteen years when I was hurt on the job and forced to resign. That is all that you need to know about me. Now, tell me a little about yourself and who you want followed."

Peter immediately liked her no-nonsense style. He just smiled when he told her his name and where he was from. Before he could answer her the receptionist entered with a cup of coffee for him. He waited for the receptionist to leave before he began. "You are not to follow anyone; I want you to find someone. Three women, Bell White, she could have married and has a different last name. Bell's sister was Sheri Albrecht, her married name. She also could have remarried, and Sheri's daughter, Candice Albrecht. Are they alive or dead, can they be reached? It is important that I to speak to one or all of them. I've heard the husband, Sheri's husband, Dannell," he spelled it so that Ms. Dix wouldn't believe that he meant Daniel, "is dead, killed in an auto accident. Is that true? Find out." As he talked Ms. Dix took notes.

Before she could ask for the particulars, she quoted him a cost per day plus expenses. It was a lot more than he had paid Rodney, but if she could do it, he wouldn't spend his time searching. She would need a fee in advance, twelve hundred dollars a week plus expenses. Peter handed her his credit card. Ms. Dix called her receptionist and told her the amount to charge and waited for the transaction to be completed. Peter signed the receipt the receptionist presented. Satisfied, Ms. Dix began, "Now, tell me about them, who they are, where I might begin looking. Anything at all about their likes, dislikes, hobbies, possible friends, what they look like."

Who they are and where they are from was easy. What they looked like and where they may be, was not. When he finished he said, "All I know is where they are, Cleveland."

"Could they be in a suburb or a local town that may be referred to as Cleveland?" she asked.

Peter didn't know. "The older of the women is Bell White, she may be dead." Should he tell her the same lie he told Mrs. White in Memphis? No. Ms. Dix didn't need to know. When she did find them, he did not think if she were found, he would need to get some of Candice's blood. He would worry about that when they were located. He had always found that money speaks louder than words. He gave the investigator all the background he could on the three he was searching for. He told Ms. Dix where he was staying, finished his coffee and Ms. Dix escorted him to her door.

Peter left and went back to his hotel room. He called Justine told her he would be home as soon as possible and wanted to know how the assignment he gave his two assistants was going. Having Justine answer what he wanted to know kept her from questioning him. When he hung up he realized he could do nothing but wait.

He bought the newspaper every day and read it from cover to cover. The three paper back novels he bought he soon read and didn't remember what he had read. He was getting anxious. The next dark of the moon was only nine days away. It would be a good day's drive or longer to Brigit de Ville which would leave him seven or possibly eight days. Plenty of time. While he was thinking this, his phone in his room rang. When he answered it was Ruby Dix. She wanted him to come to her office. She had been searching now for three days and he hoped she had good news.

When he was shown into her office she was sitting behind her desk looking at several sheets of paper. "I have good news and bad news. Which do you want first?" she asked.

"Start at the beginning and tell me what you found, both good and bad. I'm ready to hear it all," Peter replied. "Not what you did to find them, just the highlights."

She began, "They did not move to Cleveland but Barea, a small community south of the city. Dannell, the husband, was killed in a car accident. Bell and Sheri are both dead." Ms. Dix was silent for a moment.

Peter's heart sank when he asked, "And what about Candice?"

"I don't know if you want to know about her," she replied.

"Tell me it all," he said.

"As best as I could find, she became a drug addict, ran through her parent's inheritance, and spent a lot of time on the street. At some point she became pregnant, apparently her addict boyfriend was the father. Whether she married the guy or not, I was unable to find out. She gave birth to twins, a boy, and a girl. Gave them both up for adoption as soon as they were born. Shortly after that she overdosed on some bad heroin and died. The boyfriend was believed killed by a dealer. It's all written up here in my findings." She pushed her report across her desk to Peter. He did not pick it up. "I'll return the money not spent to you."

"No," Peter replied. "I want to know who adopted the twins. It is important to me." By this time he had become obsessed with what finding a relative of Sofianna.

"Those adoption records will be sealed. Difficult to open unless you have a compelling reason to do so, and it's not like you are looking for a relative," Ms. Dix told him.

"I want you to try. I must know what happened to the twins. I'll pay you extra," Peter almost pleaded.

"I will not charge you extra. Give me another week's retainer and I'll do my best," she replied.

Peter did what he was told, took the report and left her office. If he had to wait another week he would miss the next dark of the moon. If that happened he would make another trip next month to Brigit de Ville. It will be what it will be.

Back in his hotel room he read through the report. It told him in more detail what the investigator had told him. Had he reached a dead end? No. Ms. Dix would find the twins. He had faith in her. Would she be able to do it time? Peter hoped that she would.

That night he dreamed about Sofianna, her plea for help. It was almost time the dream told him. He saw the angel from hell, stared it in the face and it smiled at him. He woke before he could do anything to it or it to him. This time he was not anxious. He knew exactly what and who he was dealing with. What the dream was about and why.

It was a day later, five days until the dark of the moon, late in the afternoon when he received a call from the private investigator. She was able to track down one of the twins. Peter hurried to her office. "I won't tell you how, but I was able to locate the adoptive parents of the boy. A Mr. and Mrs. Domblinski. I was able to track them down. They moved from Cleveland to Erie. I have their address. They named their new son Donald after Donald Domblinski, the father." She again pushed her report across the desk to Peter. He quickly scanned it, thanked her, and got up to leave. "I'll continue to look for the twin girl, but I don't hold out much hope of finding her."

Peter thanked her and left. He had not reached a dead-end. He checked out of his hotel and immediately headed for Erie. He typed into his GPS Sterrettania Road, Erie, Pa. He exited I-90 onto the road. Now all he needed to do was find the address. The GPS was a big help. It was dark when he drove to the house, parked, and got out of his car. When he rang the doorbell, he could hear dogs barking, then a man yelled at the dogs. In a moment the door opened. Peter was greeted by a middle-aged man, hair down to his shoulders and sported a well-trimmed beard. "My name is Peter Frost and I would like to talk to your son, Donald. It is nothing serious, but I need to talk to him. Is he home?" Mr. Domblinski was joined by a woman close to his age and she said her name was Suzann and Donald Junior's mother. Before either could answer Peter's request to talk to their son they invited him into their home.

They offered Peter a seat and began talking. "Donald Junior is adopted. He knows it and accepts it," Suzann said.

"I know that, and this has nothing to do with the adoption or his birth parents. As far as I know, both are dead. It has something to do with his great grandmother and I am not at liberty to explain. Is he home? Can I speak to him?"

"Donald doesn't live here at home," Suzann said. "He is a design engineer for Bucyrus-Erie and lives downtown with his girlfriend. Let me call him and find out if he would like to talk to you."

She went into another room and Peter could hear her talking but could not make out the words. When she returned, she said, "My son will meet you tomorrow morning before he goes to work, at seven. Go to the McDonalds on Peninsula Drive." She explained how Peter would find Peninsula Drive and if he needed to find a motel for the night, just beyond the McDonalds, maybe a couple of hundred yards, on the opposite side of the street is a motel.

Peter followed her instructions and was able to find both. He checked into the motel and was in an upbeat mood. He thought back on how fortunate he was to hire the private investigator and now he found a descendent of Sofianna. When he got into bed he wondered how he was going to get Donald Junior to give him a sample of his blood. He would use a direct approach and offer to pay him for some. How much? Would he need a lot? Would he need a smidgen or a cup full? He didn't know. Father Thibodeaux never told him how big the cross needed to be or how clear it needed to be. When he got the blood, how was it supposed to be applied? With a brush? Dribbled on? From his finger?

The alarm in the room awakened him at six. Four days left. He showered, got dressed and drove to the restaurant. He had no idea what Donald Junior looked like. For sure there wouldn't be a resemblance to either of his parents. He most likely would be in his mid to late twenties. At a quarter to seven he entered the restaurant, it was busy. He didn't see anybody that looked like or was dressed like an engineer. But what would an engineer look like, dress like? Would he have a pocket protector and pens in it? Wear black horn-rimmed glasses? No, that was a movie cliché, he would most likely use a computer. He saw only one man by himself and he looked to be well into his fifties. Peter would wait and see who else would enter the restaurant. He ordered a cup of coffee and sat at a table and for the next ten minutes, he would watch. Immediately after he sat in the seating area, he noticed a woman and man at a table, and he believed that the woman kept looking at him. She was dressed in what he believed was a nurse's uniform with an identification badge attached to a blouse pocket. Too far away to read. He looked away but out of the corner of his eye he could see her getting up. She picked up the sweater she had draped over her chair, slipped it on and walked toward him. When she reached his table she asked, "Are you Peter Frost?"

He was surprised but said, "Yes."

"I'm Gabriel, Donald Domblinski's girlfriend. Call me Gabby. Come join us at our table." Peter grabbed his cup of coffee and followed her to their table where he met Donald Domblinski Junior.

After they shook hands, Donald said, "Mom said you wanted to talk to me, wouldn't tell me why, or about what?"

Here it was. The moment Peter had no easy answer for. He believed a simple explanation would be the best course of action to take. He began, "This has nothing to do that in any way could come back and hurt you. I've been searching for you for almost a month. I need a blood sample for your great-grandmother."

There was a surprised look on Donald's face that said are you kidding. "You want me to give you a sample of my blood for a woman I've never met and don't know?"

"Yes."

"What could she possibly want it for?" Gabby asked. "Is this to prove he really is her great grandson because of some sort of an inheritance is involved?"

Peter hesitated before he said, "No, but I'm willing to pay you for it."

"Did she hire you? Are you, us related?" Donald asked.

"Neither. She just needs it. That is all that I can say. Please," he replied. "She is old and dying and I am a friend."

"I will need a better and fuller explanation than that," Donald answered. Then as an afterthought he added, "How much? How much will you pay?"

Gabby sounded appalled when she almost yelled, "Donald!" They were all silent for a moment before she asked, "How much do you need?"

How much blood would he need? The same question he asked himself last night. Peter decided a little more of the truth was needed. He would explain and stretch the truth and see where that would get him. "Her name is Sofianna. She believes that she is possessed by the devil and was convinced by a priest that the only way of freeing herself from this demon is to be wrapped in a sheet. On the sheet a cross would need to be drawn with the blood from one of her descendants. She is old, ready to die and I want her to have a peaceful death. I don't want her to die with the last thought on her mind is that she will be going to hell. The idea that she is possessed may all be in her mind but if she sees the sheet and believes it will help her, it will."

"I've never heard of such a thing. Would this be some sort of exorcism?" Gabby asked.

"Yes," Peter replied. "Sort of," he couldn't explain any more.

"Can't you lie to her? Tell her it is a relative's blood? How would she know any different?" Donald asked.

"Take my word for it. She and the priest would know. I couldn't lie to her," Peter answered. "I have the sheet and it has already been blessed by a priest. What I need from you is the cross in blood."

"Let me think about it," Donald said, and he and his girlfriend Gabriel turned away and whispered. Peter believed that if he said yes it would be because of Gabriel.

"Come by our apartment tonight with the sheet, about seven," Gabby said.

Donald wasn't so sure but when they got up, put on their coats ready to leave, he gave Peter one of his business cards with his work and home addresses. Peter wondered if he should press Donald for the sample now. No. Better to keep it as it was, a simple blood sample to be given this evening.

That evening he went to Donald's apartment with the sheet. He showed up early in the event that Donald and Gabriel would come home early. They came home almost at seven on the dot and invited Peter into their apartment. When they took off their coats and Gabby her sweater he could see her identification badge. His original assessment of Gabby's profession was correct, she was a nurse.

"Where is the sheet?" Gabriel asked. Peter took it out from under his jacket and showed it to her. "Let's spread the sheet on the dining room table." That done she went into their kitchen and got a small first aid kit. From it she took out a small bottle of alcohol and a needle. She wiped Donald's index finger with alcohol, held his finger tightly in her hand. She would not allow him to object and stuck the end of the needle into his finger. Peter saw him flinch. As soon as she did, Peter could see blood begin to pool at the wound. Still holding his finger, Gabby drew a cross about three feet high. She let go of her husband's finger. "Is that all?" Gabby asked as she handed Donald a piece of paper towel that he held to his finger to wipe off any excess blood. Gabby next produced a band aid ready to cover Donald's cut finger.

"If it's not a bother, a second upside down cross in a circle. It can be much smaller," he told her. Gabby took hold of Donald's arm, pressed his finger to the sheet and squeezed his finger so that blood began to flow. To the best that she could she followed Peter instructions. When she finished she smiled at her boyfriend and told him it wasn't so bad. Peter was not finished. "Now extend the cross top through the circle. When she did, he told her, "Now, draw a second horizontal on the vertical outside of the circle." By this time, the image was faint, Donald's finger was bleeding less, but it was the symbol that Peter had seen so many times in his dreams and on the Albrecht's and Sofianna's doors. Gabby applied the band aid to Donald's finger and gave him a small kiss on the cheek. Told him she was proud of her big strong boyfriend. Peter thanked them both, folded the sheet and told them, "I have to leave." He turned down their invitation to stay and have dinner with them. The sooner he was on the road the better.

He would begin his drive back to Louisiana. It was only a little after eight so he believed he would be able to drive for several hours before he looked for a motel along the interstate. He had three days until the dark of the moon. Plenty of time to do what needed to be done.

Chapter 18

Peter made good time returning to Louisiana. Almost as soon as he drove west out of Erie Peter stopped at an interstate gas station and bought a map of the United States that showed all the interstate highways. That night before he went to sleep he looked at the interstate map and decided on his route. He didn't want to depend on his GPS because of what had recently happen to get him to Brigit de Ville. Sofianna's spirits caused him to drive to Brigit de Ville. Could hell's angel cause him to go off in a false direction? Was it possible that the angel knew of his plan? Knew that he had a sheet that could stop him? Peter would not chance it. He would drive to Cleveland and then south to Columbus, to Louisville and then almost straight south to Birmingham. He believed he could drive that far in one day. Early next morning, a quick breakfast, gas and he was on I-71 to Louisville and I-65 to Birmingham. The next day I-20 to I-59 to I-10. It took two days for him to reach Louisiana and interstate 10. After a solid two days of driving, he was tired. He spent the night in Metairie. Day after tomorrow would be the night of the dark of the moon.

Early next morning he drove to Brigit de Ville and checked into Cooney's hotel. Grace welcomed him back and put him in the same room as before. It was a lot warmer and it was humid and like before he opened the window, maybe a slight wind would cool the room. There was no air conditioner or sweet smell of jasmine. He believed it was going to be an early summer.

Since he left Erie he never allowed the sheet to be out of his sight or away from his person. He had purchased a small inexpensive over the shoulder man's bag at the first gas station he stopped for gas. He could carry the bag over his shoulder whenever he got out of his car. In his room he removed the sheet from the bag, unfolded it and looked at the two crosses in blood. Would it work? Yes. He was sure of it. How would he protect Sofianna from the devil's angel? Wrap her in it? Could he cover her when she was pulled to the ground? Before the angel could get at her. Could he get hurt if he tried to do it? Would the small demons, and they were demons, not spirits, be able to hurt him? Stop him? They clawed her and broke her leg, what would they do to him? He decided he would try it. While he thought about how he was going to protect her, something he had not thought about panicked him. If he were successful, how would it affect his dreams? Would it? Had he lost the purpose of his dreams? No. Helping Sofianna had become the focus of his quest. If he saved her, would his dreams stop? He believed that they would. Then a bigger question stopped him. If he were to succeed, what would happen at the next dark of the moon? Would the angel return? That aspect was not discussed with Father Thibodeaux. He could stop the angel, but not its return. Did it matter to him? Yes. Could he do anything about it? No. He would convince Sofianna to keep the sheet and wrap herself in it and the spell she cast would be broken. He would be dream free. It was the last thing he remembered before he awoke the next morning.

The questions he thought about before he fell asleep and new similar ones kept nagging at him the next day. Would the small demons be a problem? Could they help the angel? Would they claw him if he tried to protect her? If he were unsuccessful, would the angel hurt him? If he was pulled into the swamp? Is that what happened to the others Cooney talked about? The ones who never returned or were never heard of again. Had they tried to rescue Sofianna? Had they been touched by hell's angel, pulled into the swamp by its demons or were they turned into the earth with the angel? Could it happen to Peter. What if he could possibly be killed, lost like the others? One more who Beverly could talk about, et by the alligators.

If Sofianna couldn't do it after all these years could Peter convince the angel to leave her alone? How? Peter wouldn't worry about all the things from last night, the what ifs. He would just do it, for at least one night protect her. He spent the day in the town. When he went into the restaurant, Beverly welcomed him. Would he have the alligator dinner again. Because it tasted like chicken, Peter said yes, and today he would also have the pecan pie for dessert. He began to feel confident about what would happen tomorrow, so why not treat himself. Beverly recommended the pie, it may have been good, but he found it too sweet for his taste.

It was afternoon the following day and Peter drove to the large tree and parked. He thought it was more humid as he walked to Sofianna's cabin and he could smell the swamp. He was sweating when he reached it. Peter called out to her. He waited and she appeared in the open doorway and wore her glasses. Neither said anything. She joined him and together they walked into her cabin and closed the door behind them. When they were seated, she lit a candle on the table. She sat and said in an angry whisper, "Why have you returned!? Didn't I warn you to stay away!? I told you to stay away! Never to come back! Why didn't you listen to me!? Why!?"

Peter remained silent for a moment before he spoke, "I have something for you," he said and took the bed sheet from his bag.

"What is that!? Why would I want a sheet!?" she asked in a defiant whisper.

"It's more than just a sheet," and he proceeded to tell her of the power of the sheet, what she needed to do with it.

"No! Cannot do! Is dangerous!" she spit out. "I will not do it. You try to interfere, he will hurt you, kill you!" For the remainder of the day Peter tried to talk her into wrapping herself in the sheet. She would not do it. Wouldn't even consider it.

"Have you ever wished that you didn't make a deal with the angel from hell?" Peter asked after a moment of silence.

"Why you say he an angel?" she whispered.

"Because he is, he is not the devil. Father Thibodeaux told me so, and I believed him," Peter replied.

Sofianna didn't ask who Father Thibodeaux was or immediately say anything. Then in a voice that didn't challenge him she said with a note of sadness in her voice. "He is the devil to me. Reason I gave up my first born. Didn't want him to be claimed by the devil. Force me to have his son. Never knew what happened to Dannell. Didn't try to find him, if I found him, the devil would know, know where he was."

"Auntie Milly took him to Memphis where he married and later died in a small community south of Cleveland in an automobile accident," he whispered.

Sofianna was quit for a moment. "Only regret, abandoned my own chile," she said as she lowered her voice even further.

"Dannell had a daughter," Peter said. "Candice was her name."

"Maybe someday like to meet her," she uttered, the same sadness in her voice. Peter believed Sofianna was thinking of what may have been. It was too late now. She had abandoned them, and they most likely didn't know that she even existed. A relative not passed down in the family. Never seen and now forgotten.

"Can't," he said, "she is also dead."

Before he could talk about the twins Candice had, Sofianna said, "It almost dark, you should go. He will be coming soon."

Peter was just as stubborn, "No. I will not leave." He didn't tell her of his plan of covering her. If what the Albrechts said about the symbol keeping the devil out was true, the angel wouldn't, couldn't know he was in the cabin or enter it. At the last second, he would rush out and cover her. If he was to be hurt, so be it. He hoped not killed. Maybe he could lie down beside her and have the sheet cover both. They stared at each other, neither willing to give-in to the other's demands. The little light that came through the curtained window had faded; it was getting dark outside. The sounds of the swamp became louder. They heard the squeaks and squeals of the demons. Sofianna waited for the loud squeal, her signal to come outside. Peter just waited. Both were silent and determined. Neither willing to give in to the wishes of the other.

He heard squeals that were not loud and then he heard it. A very loud squeal. Sofianna got out of her seat and walked to the bedroom door and opened it. On the curtained window in the room Peter could see the fire dancing. He saw her walk through the bedroom and open the door to the outside. Light from the fire flooded into the room. Sofianna stepped through the door and he saw two of the small demons take her by her hands and begin their dance. Peter held the sheet in front of him to guarantee that the devil's angel wouldn't be able to see him. What he saw weeks before, he was seeing again, and the putrid smell of the swamp wafted into the cabin. Sofianna and the two demons were joined by other demons until the dancers encircled the fire. They began to remove her clothes and she started to become a beautiful young woman. Her body reminded him of someone, who? Donna. Except for her he had not seen a naked woman since Clare and he parted. He couldn't see Donna clearly in his bedroom, lit only from the light coming from his night light and now in the flickering light of the fire but he believed it was her. The demons may have not been real, but they did cast shadows on her which added to the uncertainty of who he was looking at. As soon as he made the decision the dance stopped. The demons formed a double row toward the swamp. He saw the angel appear like before, first as a fog or mist as it formed from the earth and swamp. It rose, covered with swamp scum. As the angel approached the fire the demons formed a circle and Peter could see like before the swamp scum drip from its head and torso, the tree roots turn into arms and legs. Also, he believed the smell of the swamp was stronger. Like before it was more than the swamp and rotting vegetation. To Peter it smelled like rotting flesh. The putrid smell seemed to sting his nose and almost caused him to throw up. When the being from the earth and swamp reached the dancers, it became more of a solid. He put the smell out of his mind. Peter watched it become more human-like and the demons continued to dance. All the remnants of the swamp had fallen off. The demons had completely undressed Sofianna. Peter saw a beautiful young Sofianna and the thought momentarily crossed his mind as to why the angel wanted her, coveted her. She was beautiful. As he watched he saw the angel try to get to her, passing the demons in its way. When it was close, the two demons who held her by her hands pulled her down and held her there. It was opposite to where Peter was on the far side of the fire. He would have to get beyond the demons and the fire between him and her. Could he run through the fire? In the past there was no evidence that the fire burned anything. Would it burn him, the sheet? He couldn't, wouldn't risk it. Could he get by the circle of demons? Would they try and stop him? Possibly hurt him with their clawed fingers? The demons broke her leg. He was not going to be able to do it. Peter was not sure he could overcome the obstacles in his way. He watched in disgust as the angel mounted her, heard the squeaks and squeals from the demons. Then, as before, the angel gave out a loud squeal. The fire began to die down and the small demons began to disappear and then most of them were gone. The moment came and now was gone. The angel knelt between Sofianna's legs turned and victoriously smiled toward the cabin and Peter. Could he be seen behind the sheet? It seemed so. The angel turned back and appeared to look at her. Was it smiling at her also? The thought upset Peter, made him angry. Without giving it any thought or what the consequences might be, or its effect, Peter rushed through the bedroom door holding the sheet in front of him. He quickly skirted the dying fire. He attempted to push aside the few remaining demons and felt no resistance. He could see them, but they were not real. He ran quickly to the angel. Peter did not know why he did it, he threw the sheet over the angel's head and pulled it tight around its neck. It struggled to get free, but Peter held it tight. He pulled back on the sheet. When he did, he saw the angel's left hand come over top of him and he felt the angel's nails bite into his head. They either couldn't or the angel didn't try to break through Peter's skull. He felt the nails instead rake down across his head and left shoulder and upper arm down to the elbow. It slashed him, cut through his shirt and flesh. One of its nails just missed his eye as it cut open the side of his face. He felt pain and could see the blood from the wounds, it ran into his eye and stung, he could feel it begin to run down his neck and chest, but he would not let go of the sheet. The angel struggled more, its arms flailing wildly back toward Peter trying to reach a vulnerable area. The more the angel struggled, the harder Peter held onto the sheet with his right harm and pulled it back toward him. But the angel would not move. Peter felt that it was stuck to the spot. His left arm hurt, hurt a lot. He could not use the left arm to hold and pull. Peter was not going to be able to use it to keep the angel trapped. Could he hold onto it with one arm? The thought flashed through Peter's mind, the angel could not see, could not free itself from the sheet and its legs had begun to turn into the earth. It was attached to the earth as it became the earth. Its hands grabbed hold of the sheet and tried to pull it off. Its claw like nails could not cut through the sheet. It may have dark powers, but it did not have strength or was it powerless against the sheet. Peter hung on. He saw its left arm come up toward him again and it swiped at his face. Peter was able to duck out of the way as the claws came near his face. He had no time to think about what to do with his captive, how he was going to get him to stop visiting Sofianna, but he was not going to let the angel go. He remembered Sofianna telling him it couldn't be bargained with. Could it be threatened? Threatened with what? Peter didn't know. He put his knee in the angels back so that he had more leverage as he pulled on the sheet. Then he felt the angel getting away from him, his knee met less resistance. He was pushing against dirt and the dirt wasn't a solid form. The angel was beginning to dissolve, get smaller as it turned into the earth. He heard squeaks and believed he could feel something pulling his shoulder, his arm. Very slight pulls. Not enough to break his hold of the sheet. He wasn't sure but believed that one or more of the demons were trying to help the angel. He had to bend over as he held onto the sheet. Peter could see in the dying fire light the angel was not getting smaller, it was disappearing further into the earth, becoming the earth. The arms below the elbows were becoming dirt. If it weren't solid could he hit an arm that had become dirt, knock it away, break through it, cause it to break apart, scatter. He would have to let go of the sheet. Peter would not take a chance, let go of the sheet. As soon as the idea passed through his mind it was too late. The arms had turned into earth and had disappeared? He kept hold of the sheet until he saw the shoulders turn to earth. It was too late. The angel was going to turn it into dirt, pull the sheet into the earth and disappear. But the sheet would not turn into dirt or be pulled into it. It would not be able to be pulled into the ground. The head under the sheet could not pass through the sheet, disappear into the earth. The sheet was stopped, stopped at the ground and so then was the angel's head. The angel was not able to completely dissolve into the earth, become the earth. Peter had it trapped if he was able to hold on. There wasn't much light from the fire, but Peter could see how bloody the sheet was now, blood from his wounds. He had lost strength in his left arm because of the slashes and now that the shock of being clawed was wearing off he began to feel more pain. Disregarding the pain, he tried to grab hold of the sheet with his left hand, but he had lost more strength in his left arm, now his arm was useless, and it hurt. He pulled as hard as he could with his right arm, pulled on the sheet and the head of the angel. It seemed like the sheet and head were attached to the ground. If it slipped out of the sheet it would get away. He was not going to allow it to get away. He was breathing hard, sweating. His strength was failing. How long would he be able to hold onto the sheet? Would he be able to keep the angel from escaping? What would he be able to do when the fire burned totally out? He was sure he could feel a demon at his side. He would not be able to fight it off. Then he saw it wasn't a demon but Sofianna beside him. What he felt was her, not a demon. She put her hands beside his, grabbed hold of the sheet. Was she going to try and free the angel? Maybe. Unable to use his left arm and her helping the angel, he would lose his battle with the angel. But he would not let go. He would fight to the last. Fight them both. As soon as Peter made the determination to fight on, he realized Sofianna wasn't trying to free the angel, she was helping Peter to hold onto the sheet and helped him pull. Between the two of them they kept the angel from escaping. Then out of his mouth he heard his words, he spoke to the angel, "I'll never let you go. Not until you break your agreement with Sofianna." It was not a bargain but a promised threat. He didn't hear it but rather felt the angel agree, it would release her. He felt Sofianna let go of the sheet and he felt it slip through his fingers and the angel was gone. He hoped gone back to hell.

It was totally dark now. The fire was gone. Had he been successful? Had he freed Sofianna from her pact with the angel? Only time would tell. Peter couldn't see anything, She and he dropped to his knees and just before he passed out, the last thing he remembered was the smell of the swamp. He would forever remember the smell, the smell of evil.

Chapter 19

Peter woke and didn't know where he was. All he could see was white and he was in bed. Was he back in Colorado? Had it snowed more? Was all that he remembered a dream? Then he could feel his head and neck were wrapped, and his left arm was bandaged, and he couldn't move his arm. He could feel what he assumed was a large band aid on the left side of his face. When he looked up he saw a nurse above him. He tried to smile at her and it hurt. "Good, you're awake," she said.

"Where am I?" he asked.

"Best as I am able to tell you, you were life flighted here to the Lafayette Surgery Center. Lucky you didn't lose an eye. Lot of stitches but our surgeons were able to save both your arm and ear. Lost a lot of blood. Don't know the details but heard you were lucky, almost killed and eaten by an alligator."

"How did I get here?" Peter wanted to know.

"That's all I know and can tell you, maybe your doctor can fill you in," she replied and left his room.

Later that day a doctor entered his room with a different nurse. She proceeded to take his temperature and checked his blood pressure. While she worked the doctor said, "I'm Doctor Sanjay, your surgeon. Hear you have questions. I'll try to fill you in. Don't know much, so can't tell you much. Man named Cooney called local parish EMs. Said a woman there told him a man at her place, attacked by an alligator. EMs found you, almost dead. They patched you up as best as possible, gave you blood and called for a life flight here to Lafayette. You were quite bit up, lost a lot of blood. Needed four units here at the center. Ear almost torn off. Arm slashed all the way to the bone. Lucky for you most of the nerves that run down your arm are on the underside and not touched. But most likely will have lost some feeling in your arm. How much will come back only time will tell. You were in surgery for well over four hours. Sewed it all together. Barely alive you lost so much blood. Don't know how a gator could have inflicted the wounds, were more like big claw slashes. No animal could have done it except for a big cat, maybe a lion. There are a few bob cats in the swamps, but they are too small to have inflicted such wounds. You must have put up one hell-of-a-fight with the gator. It tried to pull you into the water. Somehow you were able to get out of its clutches. Rushed you here and into surgery, saved your ear and left arm. Lucky your carotid artery wasn't slashed, or you would have bled out. Should regain use of your arm, like I said, don't believe any major nerves were severed but will not know until you have healed. You will have quite a few scars to remember the incident. What can you tell me about the attack?"

When Sofianna went to Cooney she had to have told him an alligator attacked him. Peter would go along with the story. No one would ever believe what really happened. His best answer to what and how it happened is going to be he doesn't remember. "Nothing. Can't remember a thing after I slipped and fell into the water. I must have hit my head," he replied.

"No evidence of a head trauma. It may come back to you with time," the doctor said. "EMTs said when they reached the old woman who found you, she led them to where you were. They patched you up and called for a helicopter. There was a large enough clearing at the woman's cabin for it to land. While they waited for it the old woman began to say some sort of incantation over you. Lot of deep bayou people believe in voodoo, magic, and spells. It wasn't a spell that saved you, but the EMTs and the doctors here at the center."

"Was there a sheet with me?" he asked the doctor.

A puzzled look was on the doctor's face when he replied, "A what? A sheet? Only the ones covering you."

"Where are they," Peter asked.

"Don't know why you are so interested in the sheets covering you. Most likely sent to the center's laundry yesterday when you were brought in," the doctor replied.

Peter did not want to hear about the sheets, but were they the ones provided by his rescuers, and not the one he had taken to Sofianna's. He hoped she kept it. Would she use it? At this point he didn't know or care. He would accept what happened at Sofianna's and if his dreams continued, he would deal with them. He knew why they occurred and the fact he couldn't do anything about them. He closed his eyes as though he had fallen asleep and he heard the doctor leave. Later that afternoon a large arrangement of flowers appeared in his room. He asked the nurse who brought them, where the flowers came from. She read to him the note that came with them, "Hope you will recover soon and get back to work, your work family, Justine and Mary Ellen?" the nurse said. "When you were checked in our admittance coordinator first contacted the guy who called the EMTs. According to the hotel sign in book he had your address but when we called got no answer. She went through your wallet and looked for an insurance card and found where you worked. She called and was told you were not married and couldn't tell about your parents. There was no one to contact. One of your assistants was told where you were and what happened."

It all made sense. He assumed Justine was calling him on his cell phone which was in his room at Cooney's hotel. Just as well. He did not wish to explain to anyone what happened. Later a second bouquet of flowers arrived with a note from his company.

Three days later, still bandaged, his arm in a sling, he was discharged. Someone in the hospital, or the hospital, had his clothes cleaned and provided him with a new shirt. Peter asked for his old shirt. His slashed left sleeve would be a reminder of what had happened. It had been destroyed. The new shirt was draped around and buttoned; the sleeve thrown over his shoulder. He had a taxi that would accept his credit card drive him to Brigit de Ville. He found that his car was still where he parked it when he walked to Sofianna's. Should he go see her? No. She had told him she never wanted to see him again. If what the doctor told him about the EMTs hearing her say an incantation over him, he hoped it was that he shouldn't die. It worked. He didn't die. If Sofianna was freed from her bargain with the devil, or one of his angels, he didn't have to help her. Only time would tell if he was dream free.

Before releasing him, Doctor Sanjay had stopped by his room, told him to take it easy for a while, not overdo anything. His body needed time to finish healing. If he was tired driving, he should stop and walk around. Rest and not push himself. The way he felt, taking it easy would be no problem.

He decided to check back into Cooney's hotel. Cooney greeted him when he returned to the hotel and wanted to know about the alligator attack. Peter repeated the same story he gave the doctor, he didn't remember a thing after he hit the water. All Cooney could say was, "Lucky you were'n et by the gator. Toll youse to stay away."

He repeated the same story when Beverly talked to him. He ate a quick meal and turned in early. His left arm would be in a sling, but he felt confident enough to drive, tomorrow he would head back to Denver.

Chapter 20

Nothing looked so good to Peter as the sign at the side of the interstate that welcomed him to Colorado. He had been gone for over two months and it was now the end of March. There was still snow on the ground. Peter didn't remember any of the trip from the border until he arrived home. He thought about not going in on Friday, take the whole weekend off. No, he would get a good night's sleep and go into his office tomorrow. One of the first things he wanted done, find Donna's address and telephone number in Los Angeles. She was sent to him, he had to find her and call. Tell her he was in the city on business, thought he would give her a call. He didn't want her to think of him as someone stalking her.

When he reached his house, he parked in his garage, entered his home, and realized he was hungry. He thawed out a frozen dinner and sat at his table to eat it when his doorbell rang. Hancock, his neighbor, was at his door. He invited him in, but Peter's neighbor declined. Hancock asked if Peter had been in an accident. His head and cheek were still bandaged, and his arm was in a sling. Peter told him it was a long story and he would talk about it some time. He was hungry and was looking forward to sleep. He asked, "What can I do for you Hancock?"

Jeffery Hancock said, "Saw you pull in, so I came over. Saturday I'm having a backyard/sunporch barbecue. Knew you didn't get an invite, weren't home, so I came over to invite you. Don't bring anything. LaToya and I will provide everything."

"It's still March, cold out," Peter replied.

"End of March, almost April. Darius is home. School vacation. Want you to talk to him about job possibilities. He seemed to listen to you in the past," Hancock said. Peter didn't respond. When he didn't say anything, Hancock added, "If you don't want to," and he hesitated, "that's alright. But please come to the cookout. LaToya will be looking forward to seeing you."

"I'll try but it's not a hundred percent guarantee," he finally replied. LaToya was a tall, well-proportioned woman and yes he thought of sex with her, but he knew he never would.

His neighbor said he hoped that Peter would make it, turned, and went away. Peter ate and went to bed. The next morning he drove to work and entered his building. Everyone he knew welcomed him back. Justine and Mary Ellen fawned over him and insisted he tell them what and how his accident happened. They knew he went to a dream clinic for help with his dreams. It was easy to describe and elaborate what he did there. When he finished his dream therapy he decided to spend time in Florida. On his way home he stopped in Louisiana. Told where he could see wild alligators, he set out by himself, slipped and fell into the water. He didn't remember anything that happened next until he woke up in a Lafayette hospital. He talked about what the doctor told him, an old woman pulled him out and saved him. There was no doubt that he was seriously hurt, he still had the bandages and arm in the sling.

When he finished, Justine asked, "What about your bad dreams?"

"Haven't had one for a while. Only time will tell," he replied and gave the impression that the dream clinic had helped him. He knew there would be further future questions. That morning, his boss as well as one after another company employee came by his office to wish him well until the morning was used up. "Time we get to work." On his desk were two stacks of envelopes. Justine had been sorting his mail and had separated it into two piles. One, correspondence that he most likely needed to respond to, the other was what she thought was junk mail, but in a day or two he should look through it before he tossed it. After she explained the two stacks of mail, Peter said, "First show me what progress you made on our expansion into medical equipment. I will want to take it home and over the weekend look at what your idea for new offices on Monday. "Justine, find out where Donna, our banquet caterer, is living and her telephone number in Los Angeles. Also see if you can find the address of a Father Thibodeaux," and he spelled the priest's name, "in Louisiana."

Peter was anxious and wanted to reconnect with Donna. Justine found her telephone number but not where she lived. He called her and she was willing to see him next weekend when he would be in Los Angeles. Justine was unable to locate where the priest lived. Peter was able to contact Rodney who was more than happy to take a half case, six fifths of bourbon to Father Thibodeaux and to thank him for the help he was to Peter. The note he should include should say it was for any chill banes the priest should encounter. And for Rodney's trouble, two cartons of cigarettes.

He looked through half of his mail, threw most of it out and began to look at his two assistants' report. He liked what he read. He put it aside and would continue this weekend at home. He was in no mood to prepare food, stopped at a restaurant and ate, and was tired when he got home. Thought he would lie down for a while. Next thing he knew it was Saturday morning and the sun was shining. During the night, like when he first regained consciousness in the hospital, no dream of his desperate woman.

Peter spent most of the day reading the report. He wrote questions or made suggestions in the margins. He dozed off and when he awoke it was beginning to get dark. Hungry, he decided to drive to a local restaurant. When he opened his garage door he saw the street full of cars and remembered Hancock's barbecue. He closed his garage door and walked to his neighbor's house. A few people asked about his accident, others accepted that he had been in an accident. Hancock had set up three overhead patio heaters and many people ate on the patio. The less hardy were in his sunroom.

As he had said, LaToya, Hancock's wife, was glad to see him. She brought him a plate in the library where Peter was talking to Darius, his neighbor's son. Darius and Peter were talking about nothing important when they soon got around to the fact that Darius would soon be graduating in less than two months with a degree in computer technology and would be on his own. First thing he would need to do was find a job. Peter told him his company used hundreds of computers. The same for other companies. Darius should check with the HR person of a company he was interested in, find out if that company needed a computer specialist, one who could be part of an IT support team, manage one, or even set one up. Darius said, "There will be companies at school recruiting after spring break. Which of these companies should I be interested in?"

"You will not know. My advice is that either you record your interviews or at the least take notes," he replied.

"Will they allow me to record the interview?"

"I don't know but let them know up front what you want to do. If they object maybe the company would not be right for you," Peter said. "Have a list of questions about things you want to know about the company," he continued.

"I know, what it will pay," Darius said.

"Salary will be important, but maybe not the most important. Work schedule, medical insurance, vacation time, where they are located and many other factors will help you decide," Peter suggested. "My advice to you is wherever you go, first thing, start a retirement saving plan or add to the plan the company endorses. Do not think that retirement is a long way off, because it will be here in a blink of an eye."

At this moment, they were interrupted by Hancock. "Sorry to interrupt but someone here wanted to know if anyone had heard from or about you. When I told her you were here, she wished to see you."

Darius thanked Peter for the advice and excused himself, got up and walked to the door. Hancock joined his son and they went back to Hancock's other guests. As soon as they were out of the room, Jannette entered. Peter began to get up. She was as beautiful as ever he thought. Maybe he would try to get her in bed. No. She would be a distraction. Tonight she wore a tight-fitting pair of jeans. There was a look of surprise on her face when she saw he was bandaged and had an arm in a sling. "What happened!?"

"A slight accident," Peter answered. "An encounter with an alligator."

"Are you alright?" she wanted to know.

"Doctor said rest and," and he hesitated, he was about to say, and a good woman was what he needed, but instead said, "time. I see my own doctor next week and he will tell me how I'm doing."

"I'm so sorry. Is there anything I can do for you?" she asked.

He shook his head no and said, "There's nothing that can be done. I'll eventually get better." She was all he needed. One more added to all the people at his company wanting to help him.

Jannette surprised him when she said something that none of the others had. "I'll kiss your owies, that'll make them better."

"My owies are my neck, side of my face, my ear and my left arm. You can't make it all better, but it was kind to offer. It may be early, but I'm tired, need to leave. Be seeing you around." He turned away from her, picked up his lightweight jacket from the chair he had been sitting in, put his right arm through the sleeve and was struggled to pull the jacket over his left arm. She went to him and helped. "Thank you." He started to leave.

"Me too, I'm going to leave. Will you walk me home?" she asked.

He believed she came with someone. It would be up to her to ditch him. Or it was possible that she only walked over since she lived so close to Hancock's house. When he was seeing Clare he often talked to Jannette and thought about getting her in bed and he was thinking it again. Was she available? Would she? The same questions he asked himself several months ago. He now concentrated on getting Donna back. Jannette may not be married but she surely would be a distraction, a problem. A problem he didn't want to deal with. He didn't say yes or no, he continued toward the door and thanked LaToya on the way out.

Outside on the sidewalk, Jannette caught up with him. He tried to walk on the outside of her, but she continued to walk on his good arm side so that occasionally her swinging hand would touch his. "You do know that a gentleman always walks on the street side of a woman," he told her. She didn't respond and they continued the short walk to her house. He stopped when they reached her sidewalk.

"You're not going to walk me to my door?" she asked.

Before he could say no, she took his hand and pulled him toward her house. She stopped at her door. She let go of his hand. Before he could turn and leave she asked, "Aren't you going to kiss me good night?"

Peter was shocked that she was so bold. Maybe he could get her in bed, but he wouldn't. He felt that he couldn't betray Donna. What immediately went through his mind was that Jannette was here to tempt him. Lure him away from Donna. Peter was sure she had been sent by Satan's angel. The angel's revenge for what Peter had done to it. He had defeated the angel once, he would not give in to this new temptation, would not be led astray. He was silent for a moment before he answered, "Jannette, we are not coming home from a date."

He was ready to leave her when she said, "If you won't kiss me," and she took his face in her hands and kissed him and when they broke apart she continued, "then I'll kiss you."

When Peter left her, he was surer that Jannette was sent by the angel to distract him, steal him away from Donna. He may, may still lust after her but he resolved to void her. Would not be tempted. She would not be able to keep him from the woman he needed.

Chapter 21

It was several months later, and Peter was driving. His bad dreams, nightmares, had stopped and he had stopped seeing his analyst. He had passed through Kearney heading east on I-80. He reached over to his disc player when Jannette's hand reached out and stopped him. "I'll change the disc," she said. On her hand was a sizeable diamond ring nested against a wedding band.

"Thought you were sleeping," he told her.

"No. Enjoying the ride and the company." She replied and pulled his hand to her lips and kissed it.

"You have had time to think about it. Are you sure you want to go through with this?" he asked her.

Without a moment's hesitation she said, "Yes." They were driving to Ohio, Pennsylvania and then to Louisiana by way of Tennessee. But first they would spend a day in Lorain. They would visit Jannette's parents, spend the night and she would show him where she had lived and grew up. Then would continue to Erie. Peter had already met her parents at his and Jannette's wedding.

Peter thought back to the events that brought them to where they were. He was looking forward to his trip to Los Angeles and meeting Donna. For the week the weather forecast was rain. A low over Denver was going to pull warm moist air up from the gulf and west Texas and Colorado could expect a lot of rain, but then a cold front was moving in from the west. When they would collide over Denver, no rain but a spring snowstorm, a blizzard in April, was expected. It would begin on Thursday and would continue through the weekend. The city should brace for a heavy snowfall. The snow began on Thursday afternoon and continued overnight and during the day on Friday. Saturday morning it was still snowing, and wind was blowing it around and created big snow drifts. The local weather forecaster said snow total was over two feet in areas and the twenty to twenty-five mile an hour wind was gusting up to sixty-one miles per hour. People were advised to stay inside and not try to travel anywhere. Most streets wouldn't be cleared for several days. The Denver mayor said that all public and private schools and the downtown area were closed. The airport canceled all flights in and out of Denver. He had to leave a message on Donna's answering machine. And would call her next week.

Peter was stuck at home. His arrangement with the lawn and tree service would remove snow for him and eventually would see that it was done. He couldn't do it and didn't know when it would be done. He had healed but his home doctor told him he should keep his arm inactive, in the sling, the stitches would come out next week. And as Doctor Sanjay told him he would have several tell-tale scars but only time would tell if he would have full use of his arm.

He looked out his window and saw his street hadn't been plowed and there was no traffic on it. He had to face it; he was marooned for the weekend. He couldn't get out. If he did, where would he go? He lit his gas fireplace, got a blanket, stretched out on his sofa and fell asleep as he thought about what he would do about food? Like everyone else in Denver, he stocked up on vital supplies, milk, bread, eggs, and several frozen dinners. A frozen dinner would have to do when his doorbell rang and woke him. His immediate thought was who could possibly be out in this weather? When he opened his door he saw Jannette standing there, all bundled up for the weather and holding a covered pot. He invited her in and when she took off her coat he got a subtle wiff of the sweet smell of her perfume. He did eventually ask her about the perfume she wore, and she told him it was a jasmine essence by Lutens. It meant nothing to him.

She had made a pot of soup and wished to share it with him because she knew he would not be able to go anywhere to eat and she didn't wish to eat alone. How was he going to get rid of her? He didn't wish to be rude, but she had to go. Peter was sure Satan's angel was behind Jannette's offer.

The two ate her vegetable soup in his dining room in front of a fire. He was halfway finished with his bowl when he remembered what Mary Ellen had told hm about eating something his neighbor, a witch, had given him to eat. And now he knew for sure that there were truly witches in the world. Was she one? Could she be? She was not from the Boston Mountains but from somewhere back east Hancock had told him. And now when the thought of her and asked himself was it possible that she could be a witch, it was too late to do anything about it. When they were finished and everything was cleaned up, she asked how long they would be snowed in. "Let's check," and he turned on the TV and tuned in the weather channel. After several minutes, the local weather forecaster said to not try to get out or drive. The city was going to be snowed in for the next several days and side residential streets would not likely be plowed for maybe a week.

"What else is on?" she asked before he could invite her to leave.

Peter began to flip through the channels. He stopped when he reached a movie, and they began to watch it. "Are you cold?" he asked her as he struggled to pull the blanket over their laps. Jannette helped and pulled the blanket up to their chins. Under the blanket she searched for his hand, found it, and held it. Peter wondered what she was doing. Why? He had often thought about having sex with her but never gave her any indication that he was attracted to her. He thought back to the brief encounters they had had. They consisted of nothing more than a hello in the morning. He was friendly toward her and that was all. But there was the kiss last weekend. Was she sending him a message? Could she be the angel's revenge? He could not, would not let it go any further.

He thought about Donna. He was supposed to be with her this weekend and here he was spending time with his divorced neighbor. Peter tried to remove his hand when she lifted it and pulled it over and around her shoulders, reached up with her free hand and took hold of it. She held him tightly to her and she leaned into him. How was he going to free himself from her?

She looked into his face and asked, "Don't you like me?" He was going to answer her when she kissed him. "Wasn't that nice?" Before he could respond he could feel that his hand was on her breast. Peter didn't remember moving his hand. It was just there. Too late and again he thought about what Mary Ellen said, eating something Jan had made. Was it possible she was a witch, had gone to one for a spell? He knew that they existed like Mary Ellen had told him. He forgot about Donna and cupped the breast. How many times had he thought about her breasts, what they would look like, feel like, as he returned her kiss. How far would she allow him to go? He didn't know. His hand moved toward the buttons on her blouse, unbuttoned the top two top and his hand was inside it and pushed under her bra and he felt her breast. He felt her move, pull away from him. She was going to stop him. Instead, she reached behind her and undid her bra fastener. He was able to now touch one or both breasts and when he moved to be in front of her he could kiss her breasts. Peter believed they were everything he thought them to be, everything he had ever imagined. She would not allow him to make love to her, remove his arm from his sling, she made love to him. He thought he heard her say she had loved him for a long time. She spent the next three days and nights at his place, and he found her to be everything he ever imagined about her. He had eaten something that she had cooked. It was too late if what Mary Ellen had said was true. But how could she be a witch? She couldn't. Would he ask her? No. And if she were one, he could not change the way he felt about her. He definitely was under her spell. The smell of her would forever excite him and at the same time gave him a calm and peacefulness that he had never known. He paid two final visits to his analyst and with her help he realized that all this time it was not lust for his neighbor but, he had been falling in love. Peter was not able to realize it because of the other pressing events in his life that occupied all his time.

That was how their romance began. He never called Donna. Jannette became enough person in his life. When he realized he was in love something he also realized, he no longer lusted after other women. He no longer wondered what a woman would look like undressed or if she would go to bed with him. Jannette was all he thought about.

The next four months seemed to pass by in a blur. He couldn't remember much of it except that he was in love and happy. His idea of expanding his company into medical equipment was going to happen. Best of all, a wonderful woman, Jannette Cotes her name before marriage, was in his life and no bad dreams.

It was two weeks after the big snow, and he began to throw out all the junk mail on his desk. He gave each piece a cursory glance before he tossed it. He did not save one piece when he was down to the last few envelops, ready to toss them when he noticed one letter had come from R. Dix Investigations. He knew why Justine put the letter in the junk mail pile. She had never heard of an investigation outfit in Cleveland. But Peter had and he believed it would be a check for money that Ruby didn't spend. Peter was partially correct. There was a check for a little over a hundred dollars and a detailed letter of her last investigation. She had continued to track down the second of Candice's twins, the girl. Ruby had found her. He read that she had been adopted by a Mrs. and Mr. Franklin Cotes of Lorain Ohio. Lorain sometimes was considered a suburb of Cleveland. Her name is Jannette. She had married a Michael Dillon of Lorain. Ruby Dix did not investigate further, if Peter wanted her to do additional investigation as to her where-abouts, she would gladly do it. The enclosed check was the money she felt she did not use. If she did not hear from Peter she would assume he was satisfied with her results and their agreement would be terminated.

Peter was shocked when he read the letter. Had Sofianna's spirits send her great granddaughter to him. She was the one he needed, not Donna.

Jannette could be a coincidence, but very, very unlikely. He would ask her where she was born. When he did, it was true. She had been adopted but considered herself to be born in Lorain. She was the great granddaughter of Sofianna. But Sofianna never knew what happened to her son Dannell so wouldn't know of any descendants or try to find them. If she did, the angel from hell would also find them and could use them to force her to bear him a son. But her spirts would know. Possibly do what was best for both Sofianna and her great granddaughter. When Peter thought about her dance with the devil, the naked body of the young Sofianna was not that of Donna but of Jannette.

When he learned the truth about Jannette, it didn't change the way Peter looked at her and the way he felt. If anything, he believed he loved her more. He kept her knowledge of her ancestors quiet. She noticed a change in him. She would often question his love. She felt there was something between them he wouldn't share with her, was it something in his past he was ashamed of? Hid from her? She assured him that no matter what had happened in his past she would accept it, him.

After they had been together for several months he decided to tell her. She most likely would not believe him but he would try. And if she left him? It would be what it would be. His two assistants didn't believe that he knew her long enough to marry her. But he knew. If they were going to be married in less than a month, she had to know. So, on a warm evening just before dark in late August they were sitting on his patio drinking iced tea when he began. "I'm going to tell you a story about me and my past that you wish to know about. Something that no one knows about. Something I've kept from you. No matter how implausible or unbelievable it may sound, don't interrupt me until I am finished." Jannette took his hand and held it tightly. She didn't know what to expect.

Peter began telling her about his terrible dreams. How he tried to find the reason for them. An analyst, seeing a group who believed in reincarnation, a medium, paying a visit to a root doctor/witch, his stay at the dream clinic, his trip to Florida to look for a fortune teller. How he got to Brigit de Ville and was to meet a real witch, Sofianna, whose voice asked for help in his dreams. How he saw her dance with the devil and what he would do in order to help her, save her and ultimately him. His trek to the bayous of Louisiana, Cleveland and Erie tracking down Sofianna's descendants and his decision to protect her with the sheet given to him by a priest with crosses of blood drawn on it by a great grandson. To all of what he was telling Jannette she just listened and squeezed his hand tighter when he came to the part where he trapped the angel from hell in the sheet and it had slashed him on his left side, not an alligator. How Sofianna helped him hold on to the unholy being. Kept it from escaping until Sofianna was freed from her pact and he from his nightmares. He had no idea how Jannette took the information that Peter told her that she was the great granddaughter of a witch and that she had a twin brother. He couldn't see her face in the darkening evening, and she remained silent even when he came to the part of his struggle with the angel from hell and his explanation of how he was hurt, and subsequent hospital stay. She knew his life from then until this day.

Peter waited for a response. She was silent. Maybe she believed he was a little crazy. Would she want him to see a, a who? Go back to his analyst? He waited. Finally, she said, "I want to meet them."

"Meet who?" he asked in the darkness.

"My brother, grandmother and great grandmother," he heard. She believed his story. "When my husband, Michael, suggested we should move to Colorado, I felt it was calling to me. I never hesitated and in less than two weeks we had moved out of our apartment and were in Denver looking at houses. He worked while I looked at houses. The day I was shown the one here, I knew it was the one. Then I saw you and your girlfriend and felt drawn to you. What had been an occasional joint on the weekend became a full-time obsession with my husband. Plus, he hooked up with a woman from his job and moved out. I knew if I waited I would eventually have you. And I do."

Chapter 22

After they left Lorain they passed through Cleveland Jannette had her eyes closed in the seat beside him. He believed that they shouldn't just drop in on Donald, brother or not. Jannette might upset his life. He should call and warn him and his girlfriend. Jannette agreed and so he called before they left her parents in Lorain. Gabby answered and said Donald was at a meeting and couldn't talk to him. When he told her who they were and of their plans she said she would talk with Donald and find out if it would be okay. They were driving to Erie when his cell phone buzzed. Jannette answered and he heard her talk to Gabby. They talked for five minutes before she hung up. It was okay with Donald and they should come to their apartment at close to four in the afternoon. Donald would come home early. "She sounded awfully nice," Jannette said.

They arrived at the designated time. Gabby answered the door, introduced herself and invited them in where they not only met Donald but also his adoptive parents, Mr. and Mrs. Domblinski. Gabby had prepared dinner for all of them, so they had to stay, and the brother and sister spent the time finding out a little about each other. They stayed until well after midnight. After Mrs. and Mr. Domblinski left, Gabby asked about the sheet. During their talk, neither he nor Jannette talked about Sofianna and the fact that she was a witch. "I can't tell you anything because my friend didn't die, and I believe to this day she still has the sheet. I've never asked her."

The next day they were passing through Cleveland when he asked Jannette if she wished to stop and see her parents again. No. Almost to Memphis when they stopped for the night at a motel. Peter felt the same way about Jannette's grandmother, Mrs. White. They could find out where she lived but he felt it better to call and again not just show up. Mrs. White did not want to meet them. She had cut off all communication with her daughters, Sheri, and Bell, and was still angry with them. Wanted nothing to do with a granddaughter and would not give Jannette, her address. If they showed up, they would not be welcome.

Peter and Jannette talked it over and decided that her grandmother was quite dead set on not wanting to meet her. It saddened Jannette but they would not pursue it. The fact she didn't wish to meet her granddaughter saddened Jannette, but she was willing to accept it. She did give Mrs. White their phone number if she ever changed her mind.

Next morning they were on their way to Louisiana. When they reached Brigit de Ville, they stayed in Cooney's hotel. There was no way they would be able to contact Sofianna. Peter believed he could go to her and find out if she would meet with her great granddaughter.

"No," replied Jannette as she talked over breakfast at Cooney's diner, "I want, to see her, whether or not she wants to see me. If what you told me about her, living alone out in the swamp, I can't upset her life and she is so much a part of your life. It was because of her and you said her spirits that we are together. I think I want to thank her."

"You can if hell's angel has not let her go. He could use you to force her to do something she has been able to say no to for decades," he replied.

Jannette listened to him but after a while she said, "She has not come to you in your dreams and ask for help. The spell she made has been broken. The angel has left her alone."

There wasn't the least hint of doubt in her voice, she was intent on meeting her great grandmother. Peter wasn't going to be able to convince her otherwise. Cooney interrupted their breakfast when he said hello to Peter. Peter introduced Jannette to Cooney but not her relationship to

Sofianna. Jannette invited him to join them for breakfast, at least have a cup of coffee with them. He sat, grabbed a cup from a nearby table and poured a cup of coffee from their carafe. He looked at Peter and spoke, "Youse havn't learned youse lesson bout da swamp. Youse two gonna go see da witch? Say way from da water, gators mean an hungry this time of year." Cooney thanked them for the coffee, left over a half cup, got up and said as he was leaving their table, "They get hold of youse again, not let go."

When he was gone Janette asked, "Everyone around here believe she is a witch?"

All that Peter could utter was, "Yes," as Cooney began to leave their table. Jannette could see Cooney give his head a slight nod yes as he heard both their comments. After he had gone, Peter followed up with, "People around here are afraid of her. Some will go to her for a spell."

It was after lunch when Peter and Jannette were walking toward Sofianna's cabin. Jannette complained about the heat, humidity, and smell. "I hardly notice any smell. Nothing we can do about the heat and humidity," replied Peter. "Like that down her. After all, we are in the middle of a big swamp."

There it was. Through the trees they could see the cabin. As they approached it Peter could see Sofianna seated in her chair on the porch and she was fanning herself. "What I do fer you dis time?" she asked. No whispering this time.

There was no way he was going to be able to talk Jannette out of the meeting, so he decided to face the fact head-on. "I've brought someone to meet you, the woman I needed, my wife." He stepped to the side and indicated Jannette with his hand, "Sofianna, I want you to meet my wife, your great granddaughter, Jannette. Jannette this is your great grandmother." Both women were quiet. Sofianna got up from her chair and stepped off the porch, Jannette took a step toward her. They stopped when they were an arm's length apart. Peter didn't know what was going to happen. He could see a tear begin to form in the corner of Sofianna's eye. Suddenly Jannette threw her arms around Sofianna and she hugged her. "I'm so very glad to meet you great grandma," she said.

Sofianna was unable to speak but Peter could see tears began to roll down both cheeks. She never questioned Peter about her great granddaughter. If he said it was so, it was so. He had never told her an untruth. Sofianna and Jannette began talking as though they were long lost friends. Neither knew anything about their closest relatives so Jannette was told about many of her now dead relatives and she in turn talked about her life, friends, school, her twin brother, Sofianna's great grandson, and of course, her new husband, Peter. As they talked Peter drifted off. The next thing he knew was that Jannette was waking him and he realized that more than several hours had passed. The two women had talked themselves out.

It was a bit of a surprise when he heard Jannette tell him, "Great grandmother is going to quit casting spells and any other witch stuff she used to do because she's coming to live with us in Denver. She will not need to do any of that stuff."

Peter didn't ask how Jannette talked Sofianna into it but as soon as he heard her say it, he believed it was to be expected and so he accepted it. Sofianna's willingness and ability to make such a radical life-time change was never brought up. He found two men in the next town over who had a box truck and would gladly move Sofianna's stuff to Denver. For their time, labor, and use of their truck, Peter was going to pay them two thousand dollars and an additional four hundred dollars each for food and motel stays. He was so willing to pay them they also said gas would be extra. Before he could say anything Jannette told them okay. For the two following days they helped Sofianna pack what she wanted to take with her. There was little so that when Peter saw the amount, he had the guys with the truck take it all in a pickup truck and covered with a tarp. Peter removed one of the doors with the symbol carved on it and included it. It would be the door to his patio. It would not be used to keep the devil out but to remind Peter of all that had happened recently in his life to bring him to where he was now. Sofianna, with the help from Jannette, repotted many of her garden plants which took up most of the first day and she would take them with her when she was in the air-conditioned car with Peter and Jannette. They took up one side of the backseat floor and several were on the seat in a wooden box. In Peter's back yard she would plant a small garden with Jannette's help. Three days after it was decided that she would live with them in Denver, they had an early breakfast in Cooney's diner, and they set off for Colorado.

The End